KRISTY AND THE NASTY NAPPIES

A big box was waiting for me when I got home from school that day. On it was the Natt's Nappies logo.

"Uniforms for the Krushers!" I reached inside and pulled out one of the shirts. It was soft. It had that great, new-clothes smell.

And it had the Natt's Nappies logo printed on it.

That was it. Just two words and the drawing.

Nowhere did it say Kristy's Krushers.

How could I stand seeing my team wearing these? How could *I* wear a uniform like this?

KRISTY AND THE NASTY NAPPIES

Ann M. Martin

Scholastic Children's Books,
Commonwealth House, 1–19 New Oxford Street,
London, WC1A 1NU, UK
A division of Scholastic Ltd
London ~ New York ~ Toronto ~ Sydney ~ Auckland

First published in the US by Scholastic Inc., 1995
First published in the UK by Scholastic Ltd, 1998

ISBN 0 590 19644 8

Typeset by Rowland Phototypesetting Ltd,
Bury St Edmunds, Suffolk
Printed by
Caledonian International Book Manufacturing Ltd, Glasgow.

10 9 8 7 6 5 4 3 2 1

*The author gratefully acknowledges
Peter Lerangis
for his help in
preparing this manuscript.*

1st CHAPTER

"Whoa! Feeeess, Kristy!" my brother David Michael called.

Well, that's what it sounded like. It was hard to tell what he was saying.

Whack! Thump! Whirrrrrrr! went the builders two houses away.

Eeeeeeeeee! droned the cicadas in the trees in the garden.

I was in the garage, gathering up softball equipment. It was a hot, noisy Friday morning at the end of the summer, four days before the start of school and eight days before the World Series. *Our* World Series, that is. You see, I'm founder, manager and head coach of a team called Kristy's Krushers. The team is named after me, Kristy Thomas.

"Kristyyyyyy!"

I looked out of the garage door, towards

1

the back of my house. David Michael was scampering towards me, grinning.

Clatter-clatter, bang, crash! Four aluminium bats fell to the garage floor. One of them smashed me on the left big toe.

"Yeeeeow!" I yelled.

"Kristyyyy!" David Michael shouted again.

I did not have a fit. I kept my cool. I stood up and calmly replied, "*WHAT?*"

Picture the Road Runner stopping short and leaving skid marks behind him. That was my brother.

"Why are you yelling?" he asked.

"I am not yelling!" I yelled.

"Why are the bats on the floor?"

Whaack! Thump! Whirrrrrrr! the builders answered. The cicadas hummed along.

It was one of those days!

I'd been having a lot of "those days" recently. The cicadas had been at it since the beginning of August. (Do your neighbourhood trees have them? They are so noisy!) The builders had started a couple of weeks later. I am convinced they go to noise-training classes. Each morning at seven-thirty sharp the banging began, along with the buzzing, beeping, drilling and shouting. I'd stopped setting my alarm. I didn't need it any more.

I am usually an early bird. And, to tell the truth, I can be pretty noisy myself. (Just ask my friends.) But this was going too far.

I couldn't wait to start a nice, peaceful softball practice.

David Michael was flexing his arm in front of my face. His teeth were gritted. "Feel this, Kristy," he grunted, nodding at his biceps.

Well, *biceps* was a strong word. *Bump* was more like it. David Michael is seven years old.

Sighing, I wrapped my hand around his skinny little arm and squeezed. "Wow!" I tried to sound enthusiastic, but it wasn't easy. I was thinking about my sore toe, the garage floor strewn with bats, and the fact that practice began in ten minutes.

And I hate hate *hate* lateness.

"I am really strong!" David Michael exclaimed.

"You certainly are. I wonder how many bats you can carry to the field."

That did it. David Michael bent down and scooped up three of the bats. As he lumbered out of the garage, huffing and puffing, the bats waggled up and down. "See?" he said.

"Fantastic!" I let him have his moment of glory.

3

Around another bat I looped the handles of our worn out equipment duffel bag (which contains balls; an old, taped-up plastic batting tee; a wrench; insulating tape; a first-aid kit; a batting helmet and a few gloves). I rested the bat on my shoulder, so the bag hung over my back. Then I followed my brother down the drive.

By now you've probably noticed how nice I was to David Michael. I complimented him on his "muscle". I didn't yell at him for distracting me. I didn't talk back when he acted superior. Do you know why? It's not that I'm the world's most patient, wise and loving person. (Well, I'm close, but that's not it.)

It's training.

You see, kids are my business. I know that sounds daft, but it's true. I founded the Babysitters Club, or BSC, and we are about the most kid-friendly, kid-knowledgeable group in the greater Southern Connecticut area.

My BSC friends call me an Ideas Machine. I don't know about the Machine part, but the Ideas part is true.

For example: you've probably already guessed that I'm a sports-lover. Well, I noticed that some of our BSC charges enjoyed softball, but they weren't ready for Little League.

Would I let them be doomed to sit around, moping, never learning the finer points of our national pastime? No way.

Kristy's Krushers were born.

How is the team? Pretty bad, if you want to know the truth. But the idea is to have fun and learn basic skills, that's all.

Of course, demolishing Bart's Bashers in the World Series would be nice, too.

Did I mention that I'm rather competitive? I am. (So's Bart. Bart Taylor, that is. Even though our teams are rivals, he's kind of my boyfriend. So as you can see, my competitiveness isn't *too* out of control.)

Before I go on, you should probably know a few other things about me. I'm thirteen, and five feet tall. I'm in the eighth grade at Stoneybrook Middle School. I have brown eyes and long brown hair. I never wear face paint (er, make-up), and my earlobes have not been stabbed (er, pierced). I wear comfortable, casual clothes all the time. If that's not enough to pick me out of a crowd, I'm the one who talks a lot and has the strongest opinions.

My life is pretty complicated and fascinating. (Well, it is.) I live in a mansion with my mother, stepfather, three brothers, a stepsister and stepbrother, an adopted sister, my grandmother and a few pets.

My stepdad, Watson Brewer, is a millionaire. But Watson is nice and quiet and normal. His two kids from his first marriage live with us during alternate months. (Karen is seven and Andrew is four.)

You already know my younger brother, David Michael. My two older ones are Charlie, who's seventeen, and Sam, who's fifteen. My adopted sister, Emily Michelle, also known as The Sweetest Girl in the World, is two and a half years old. She's from Vietnam, but she's learning English words fast these days. (At the last Krushers practice, she kept yelling "Strike one!" every time I swung the bat.) When Mum and Watson adopted her, Nannie (my mum's mum) moved in with us to help out with Emily Michelle.

I can't leave out Boo-Boo, or he'd sulk. Boo-Boo is Watson's cranky, fat, old cat. He tolerates David Michael's Bernese mountain dog puppy, Shannon, who is an enormous fluff of brown and white. Bob the hermit crab and Emily Junior the rat (yes, rat) travel up and down with Andrew and Karen, who also have two goldfish called Goldfishie and Crystal Light the Second that they keep at our house.

Don't visit our house if you're looking for peace and quiet. It's pretty wild, as far as huge, nine-bedroom mansions go.

Before Mum married Watson, she and my three brothers and I lived in an average-sized house on Bradford Court. My dad used to live there, too, but he abandoned us just after David Michael was born. That, I promise, is all I will mention about my father. Frankly, I don't like talking about him.

Back to the day of the softball practice.

I could tell it was going to be hot. I started sweating the moment David Michael and I reached the pavement.

"I want to watch the destruction workers!" David Michael said.

"*Con*struction," I corrected him.

"No. You should see the front wall."

We were supposed to cross the road to pick up a couple of the other Krushers, Linny and Hannie Papadakis. But David Michael had made me curious.

We made a detour past the house of our nextdoor neighbour, Mrs Porter. Then we saw the house next to hers. Sure enough, the whole of the front wall had been bashed in, leaving only the beams.

"See?" David Michael said. "That's *de*struction. They're tearing the house down."

"If they were, why would they be putting an extension on the side?" I asked.

David Michael scratched his head. "Maybe that's for the workers to live in while they bash the house down."

"Uh-huh. Right."

New neighbours. I was so excited. The house had been empty for ages. I was dying to find out who was moving in. Maybe they had kids.

The Krushers were in desperate need of a shortstop.

We crossed the road to the Papadakises' house.

"Yo! Big D!" Linny greeted David Michael through the front screen door. "My mum's packing us some *koulourakia* to take to practice."

David Michael jumped up and cried, "All *right*!"

To me, what Linny was referring to sounded like some strange Mediterranean disease. It's not. You see, the Papadakises are Greek, and *koulourakia* are a kind of Greek biscuit. They're good, too. We began eating them on the way to the field.

"Doo Haw havoo pay thuh bay," Linny said, spraying crumbs.

"Swallow, please," I interrupted.

He did. "Does Hannie have to play third base? If she does, I won't play."

"I want to," Hannie protested.

Linny shook his head. "You throw like a girl."

"I *am* a girl!"

"That's no excuse!"

"Ahem, who's the coach of this team?" I asked.

That quietened Linny down. He can be bossy, especially with his little sister (he's nine and she's seven).

"Linny, feel my muscle," David Michael piped up, flexing his arms as he lifted the bats.

"That's nothing," Linny replied. "Feel mine."

The four of us compared biceps all the way to the official Krusher playing field, otherwise known as the Stoneybrook Elementary School grounds.

By the time we arrived, the bodybuilders had given me all four bats to carry. As I put everything down behind home plate, I called out, "Line up for catch!"

David Michael, Linny and Hannie scurried off for their gloves. They moved

9

a few metres away from me and spread apart.

"Pop fly!" Linny demanded.

I lobbed a high one.

"I've got it! I've got it! I've got it!" Linny yelled.

He didn't. The ball plopped to the ground and rolled towards second base. David Michael and Linny both dived for it, but it rolled away and came to a stop at Hannie's feet. She picked up the ball and carefully dusted it off. Then she threw it past the foul line, between home and first.

Once upon a time, the spectators' benches would have stopped that ball from rolling away. But they had been destroyed during a summer storm, so the ball had a nice, open run.

I had to do a hundred-metre dash to track it down.

"Oops!" Hannie said.

Welcome to Krusher practice.

"A little rusty, but that's okay!" I called as I ran back. "Ground ball, David Michael!"

I threw a bouncer. My brother squatted and waited.

"Touch your glove to the ground!" I warned him.

Did he listen? No. He watched the ball

approach. He watched it go under his glove. Then he bent over and watched it through his legs.

My brother, the ostrich.

I expected *someone* to run after the ball. But Linny and Hannie were looking the other way.

They were waving at Buddy and Suzi Barrett, who had just arrived with Shannon Kilbourne. (Shannon's a BSC member.)

"Watch it, Kris—" Shannon cried out.

Thud! The softball whacked me on the left arm.

"Sorry," David Michael squeaked.

"Are you okay?" Shannon asked.

"Yeah," I said. "He didn't throw it that hard."

"I did!" David Michael insisted.

"Oh, okay, Owwww!" I cried.

Shannon burst out laughing. David Michael smiled proudly.

Soon Bobby Gianelli arrived with his mum, and Jackie Rodowsky with his dad. They're both seven (Bobby and Jackie, not their parents).

By ten o'clock, every team member was on the field. That's right, ladies and gentlemen, *your* Krrrristy's Krrrrrushers ... ushers ... ushers! (Imagine a loudspeaker with lots of echo.) And here was the day's lineup: Leading us in seniority was our nine-year-old, Linny. Our seasoned and strong eight-year-olds included Nicky Pike, Jake Kuhn and the famous Buddy Barrett. Filling out the team at seven years of age (along with Bobby, David Michael, Jackie and Hannie) were Matt Braddock, Margo Pike and the irrepressible Karen Brewer. Following them was our lone six-year-old, Laurel Kuhn, and our fabulous fives— Claire Pike, Suzi Barrett, Patsy Kuhn and Myriah Perkins. Four-year-olds Andrew Brewer, Jamie Newton and Nina Marshall brought us into the junior territory, surpassed in youth only by Gabbie Perkins at a tender two-and-a-half.

(Do you think I should be a sports reporter? I'm seriously thinking about it.)

The field was full of kids, parents and babysitters. Some parents had brought snacks and drinks. Karen's and Andrew's stepdad, Seth, was there. (Our families are friendly. Seth's a nice guy.)

Shannon and I gave the kids a workout. We fed them a steady stream of fly balls and grounders. We made them run the bases. We matched them up for games of catch. We put together the tee (with some insulating tape) and organized batting practice.

12

How did it go? Well, the kids tried hard. They were really excited about the World Series. I kept yelling "Excellent!" and "Looking good!" even when it wasn't and they weren't.

Suzi kept dropping the ball during catch. When Buddy laughed at her, she threw a tantrum and hid behind a maple tree for most of the practice.

Linny actually hit the ball out of the infield once. He insisted on doing a "home run trot", pumping his fists and waving to the crowd in slow-motion. *Super* slow-motion. So slow, in fact, that Nicky managed to tag him out.

Gabbie, our only player who's allowed to hit a plastic ball, gave up after six swings and decided to play with her train set in the dirt.

Jackie ate so many Jaffa Cakes he nearly threw up on the basepaths. Jake decided to try wearing his glove on his head and fielding with his hat. Claire hid a ball in her shirt. Andrew and Jamie found a praying mantis and followed it around the field.

We had a *long* way to go.

Shannon must have sensed I was concerned. Towards the end of practice, she whispered to me, "I. O. A. G."

"What's that?" I asked.

"It's Only A Game," she replied.

No, it's not, I wanted to say. *It's a series.*

Well, it's true. Best of five games wins the championship. So it's not "only a game".

But I kept my mouth shut. I smiled. I knew what she meant.

After practice I was sweaty and exhausted. As I walked home, my arms ached from the weight of the bats.

Shannon and the Kuhn kids walked home with us. (Mrs Kuhn was going to pick up Jake, Laurel, and Patsy from Shannon's house.) Jake and Linny were throwing the ball to each other, racing after each missed catch. Patsy and Hannie were playing some unrecognizable form of tag.

"They have so much energy left over," Shannon remarked.

"They shouldn't," I grumbled. "Not if they'd given one hundred per cent in practice."

"Mm-hm." Shannon was humouring me.

Let me tell you, being a leader isn't easy.

I knew it was lunchtime as we approached my neighbourhood. I didn't even have to look at my watch. Why?

Because the builders were quiet as mice. Eating is the only thing that makes them put down their tools.

The house was still missing its front wall. But this time, as we passed, a dark-haired woman in khaki trousers and a white cotton shirt emerged from the house. She was holding a clipboard.

"Is that our new neighbour?" David Michael asked.

"Has she got any children?" Hannie piped up.

"Ask her," I suggested.

David Michael put on his shy face. "No, *you* ask."

Linny rolled his eyes. "'Scuse me, have you got any children?"

The woman turned. She gave Linny a funny look for a moment, then smiled. "Oh! You think . . . no, I'm not . . . I'm the decorator."

Laurel looked shocked. "Aren't you angry with them for wrecking the house?"

The woman laughed. "I understand they're going to repair it. Are you all neighbours?"

"Except for Jake and Patsy and Laurel," David Michael informed her. "They're aliens."

"Hey!" Patsy protested.

"It *means* people from another place," David Michael shot back.

I quickly cut off that line of conversation and introduced us.

"I'm Sylvia Steinert," she said. "I suppose you wouldn't mind having some more playmates in the neighbourhood, would you?"

Playmates? That meant more kids. I'd have to slip a BSC leaflet under the door. And I'd need their phone number. Then I could call to offer babysitting help during the move . . .

"How old?" Hannie asked.

"Twelve or thirteen, I believe," Miss Steinert replied, looking at her watch. "They're twin girls."

"Cool!" Hannie said.

"Old girls," Linny muttered. "Yuck!"

"Uh, beg your pardon?" I said.

Giggling, Linny tore off towards his house. The other kids ran after him.

Shannon and I said goodbye to Miss Steinert and followed the kids.

Twin girls, our age, in the neighbourhood? It was the best news I'd heard all day.

2nd CHAPTER

"This meeting will—"

Rrrrrring! The phone cut me off at the moment Claudia Kishi's clock clicked to five-thirty.

"First call of the school year!" Claudia cried.

"—come to order!" I finished.

Claudia's hand paused over the receiver. "Hmmm. I bet it's the Kormans."

"Uh-uh, Mrs Prezzioso!" Jessi Ramsey said. "Yesterday she told me—"

"The Hobarts," Stacey McGill guessed.

Rrrrrring!

Claudia picked up the receiver. "Baby-sitters Club!" she said. "Fine, thanks, Mrs Hobart, and how was *your* summer?"

"I knew it!" Stacey said.

17

We were in business.

It was Wednesday, the second day of school. Everyone had arrived early for the meeting. Until the phone rang, we hadn't stopped talking about the summer—who did what, who went where. If you think about that, it's pretty funny. I mean, we'd been together a lot. Each of us knew what the others had done. We'd held meetings, babysat, gone on trips together, you name it.

But did that stop us? No way. We just repeated everything and *still* laughed our heads off.

Oh well, what good is September if you can't reminisce about the summer?

"Uh-huh. . . Okay, I'll call you back," Claudia said. She hung up and turned to Mary Anne Spier. "Monday after school?"

Mary Anne opened the club record book. "Let's see, Stacey and I are free."

"I sat for them last time," Stacey said. "You go ahead."

"All right," Mary Anne replied.

Claudia tapped out the Hobarts' number.

Efficient, isn't it? Everything organized, every duty taken care of. A well-oiled machine, that's the Babysitters Club.

Okay, sorry, I'm bragging. You see, I

invented the BSC. The basic idea: to enable Stoneybrook parents to fill all their babysitting needs with one phone call.

That's it. Simple, isn't it? So how come no one else ever thought of it? Beats me. The idea popped into my head one day when my mum spent forever calling all over town for a babysitter for David Michael. (My older brothers and I were busy.) She didn't find one, and I felt sorry for her. It seemed so unfair. I mean, you get services for finding just about everything—concert tickets, taxis, flowers, food, clothes—so why not babysitters?

Click! I had the idea. Mary Anne and Claudia were the first people I asked to join the club. Stacey joined soon after, and then Dawn Schafer. As we became busier, we took in Jessi Ramsey, Mallory Pike, Shannon Kilbourne and Logan Bruno.

If you were keeping count, you know that meant we had nine members. But we're down to eight now, because Dawn moved back to California. (How do I feel about that? Not great, but I'll tell you about it later.)

First things first. Here's how the club works. We meet three times a week, on Monday, Wednesday and Friday, from five-thirty (sharp) to six o'clock in

Claudia's bedroom. She's the only member with a private phone line, which doubles as the official BSC number. Stoneybrook parents call during that half hour to arrange sitting appointments.

Room. Phone. Sitters. The set-up was easy. Making it work was something else. First we had to attract clients. To do that, we put up ads and handed out leaflets.

Then we had to *keep* the clients. Would parents be turned off by too many sitters? I know I would, if I had to break in someone new each time I booked a sitter. I decided that everyone should write a description of each job in a notebook, so we could learn from one another about our clients. I invented Kid-Kits, which are boxes of our old toys, games, books and child-related stuff that sitters can take to jobs. I also made sure we had a strong, reliable organization with rules, officers and record-keeping, like a real company.

I'm the chairman. Basically I'm in charge of the Big Picture. I run the meetings. I dream up events for our charges. I think of ways to increase publicity. I keep my eye on the future of the BSC.

But you've heard enough about me. On to Claudia, our vice-chairman. As we use her number, she has to answer the phone whenever clients phone during non-meeting hours. That's her only official function. Her unofficial function is extremely important. You might call Claud our Club Caterer. Junk-Food Caterer, that is.

After returning the Hobarts' call, Claudia cried, "Time to celebrate! I have this bag of mini-Snickers. . ."

She hopped off her bed and scooted over to the wardrobe. Standing on her toes, she reached towards the back of her shelf, behind her hats.

She pulled out a dusty bag of popcorn.

"Oh!" She groaned. "I spent an hour looking for this last Halloween."

"I love popcorn," I said.

"That's almost a year old!" Jessi remarked.

"So? Sugar doesn't go off." Claudia ripped the bag open. "Ah! It still has its full flavour bouquet."

Well, I just lost it. I fell off my director's chair, laughing.

Claud's funny. She is also the thinnest junk food addict in the whole world. You'd think she was one of those models who eat dandelions and organic swamp-grass (or whatever) all day. Claudia doesn't have any spots, either, despite all the chocolate. She has gorgeous, almond-shaped eyes and deep, raven black

21

hair. She's second-generation Japanese-American by the way, which means her grandparents immigrated to the United States.

Mr and Mrs Kishi are super-strict about healthy food. If they knew what Claudia really ate, forget it. They'd have a heart attack. Biscuits, sweets, crisps, pretzels—Claud could open a sweetshop in her room. But you'd never know it, because she hides it all so well. She also has to hide other terrible, forbidden things: Nancy Drew books. Yes, Claud's addicted to them too, and yes, her parents disapprove of them. They would rather Claudia read only the classics. (Personally I think this is daft. I mean, there's nothing wrong with *Oliver Twist* and stuff, but my life would be miserable without sports books.)

Unfortunately, Claudia's older sister, Janine, sets a bad example. She's a brilliant student. Claud isn't, by a long shot. Her grades are mediocre (and her spelling is horrible). My scientific theory is that Claudia actually does have the Kishi genius genes. They just took a wrong turn—tripped over the junk-food-loving DNA or something—and ended up in the "art" part of the brain. Claudia has a magic touch with anything artistic—

drawing, jewellery-making, sculpting, painting. Even fashion. She puts together outfits from stuff she buys at garage sales and charity shops. She picks junk you think she'd never wear. But she does, always in some incredibly cool, funky combination.

Claudia is one of my two oldest friends. The other is Mary Anne. We all grew up on the same street.

Mary Anne also happens to be my best friend. We even look somewhat alike. She's also short and has brown hair and brown eyes. Like me, she was brought up by a single parent, her dad. (Mrs Spier died when Mary Anne was a baby.) The similarities end there, though. For one thing, she hates sport. For another, she's shy. And she cries at the slightest thing. She actually wept reading a Dr Seuss book to Andrew Brewer. (Absolutely true. It was *The Lorax*.) Her boyfriend, Logan Bruno, keeps saying she should wear a raincoat when she watches sad films.

Since Dawn Schafer moved away, Mary Anne's been especially sad. They're not only stepsisters, but they brought their parents together. When Dawn moved to Stoneybrook from California (with her brother and divorced mum), she and Mary Anne discovered that Mrs Schafer and Mr Spier had been highschool sweethearts. So the two girls played matchmaker, and it worked! Having siblings changed Mary Anne's life. She'd been an only child, and her dad had brought her up with all these strict rules. (He went overboard, trying to be a perfect parent.) Marriage loosened him up a lot, and now Mary Anne's allowed to dress and act her age.

Mary Anne is a great club secretary. Her job is to keep the record book. When a call comes in, she needs to know exactly who's available. (That means keeping track of all our commitments—ballet classes, art lessons, doctor's appointments, after-school activities, blah blah blah.) Then she helps assign the job, making sure everyone does a roughly equal amount of work. She carefully records each job on a master calendar. In the back of the book, she keeps an up-to-date client list: addresses, phone numbers, rates paid and any special information about the kids.

(Can you imagine doing all that and not going crazy? Mary Anne *enjoys* it.)

Our club treasurer is Stacey McGill, mainly because she actually likes maths. Every Monday she collects subs. She makes sure we contribute to Claudia's phone bill and give my brother Charlie petrol money for driving me to meetings. Also, she sets aside funds for our special events, which occasionally include pizza parties for ourselves.

Stacey always looks great. She'll turn up at school in a wild outfit you never saw before, and the next month it'll be on some model on the cover of *Just Seventeen*. It's amazing how she does that. She also has curly, golden-blonde hair and a smile straight out of a TV ad.

Like Dawn and me, Stacey's a child of divorced parents. She grew up in New York City, until her dad's job moved him to Stoneybrook. Then, after she'd joined the BSC, the company moved him back to NYC (that was when we took to Jessi and Mal). When her parents split up, Stacey was given the choice of living with her dad in New York or with her mum in Stoneybrook. Stacey is crazy about the Big Apple. She thinks it's the centre of the world. But she chose Stoneybrook, because that's where her absolute best, loyalest, most high-quality friends are (ahem)!

You know what amazes me? Stacey does not touch the sweets at a BSC meeting. True, she's not allowed to, as she's a diabetic, which means her body doesn't metabolize sugar (she even has to inject herself every day with a drug called insulin). But still, the temptation! I'd go crazy. She's perfectly happy with pretzels and crisps.

Stacey, by the way, is earning her way back into the BSC. You see, I had thrown her out. Honest! She'd been missing meetings and swapping jobs at the last minute, and treating the other members badly, just because she wanted to spend more time with her boyfriend, Robert Brewster. Anyway, she eventually came to her senses and asked to rejoin. I said we'd experiment for a while, play it by ear. So far, luckily, she's been behaving just fine.

Every BSC member I've discussed so far is thirteen years old and in eighth grade. Jess and Mallory, whom we call our junior officers, are eleven and in sixth. They are best friends, and both are horse fanatics. They're also the oldest kids in their families, and they love moaning about how their parents still treat them like babies. (For one thing, neither of them is allowed to take evening babysitting jobs, except for their own families.)

Jessi is African-American. (You would not believe how prejudiced some Stoneybrook people were when her family moved to town. Honestly, it was disgusting.) Her parents are *not* divorced, and she has an eight-year-old sister called Becca and a baby brother called Squirt. Jessi, by the way, is a great ballerina. Even I can tell, and to me watching ballet is about as much fun as eating beans.

Mallory is Caucasian, and her family is huge (eight kids altogether, including boy triplets). She has thick brownish-red hair and glasses, and she loves writing and illustrating her own stories. It's probably the only way she can have some peace and quiet in her house.

The BSC includes two associate members, Shannon Kilbourne and Mary Anne's boyfriend, Logan. Shannon's blonde and blue-eyed and really energetic. She goes to a private school called Stoneybrook Day, where she is involved in lots of extracurricular activities. Logan's quite a sports fanatic. He's in the Stoneybrook Middle School football, baseball, volleyball and track teams. He has curly blondish-brown hair and a lovely smile. Neither Logan nor Shannon is required to attend meetings or pay subs, but we depend on them for overflow jobs, and we ask them to fill in for absent members.

For example, Shannon once filled in as a regular member when Dawn left for a long trip to California. I was kind of hoping she'd do it again now. But I wasn't holding my breath. Shannon had phoned earlier to say she had to miss the meeting. When I'd hinted about Dawn, Shannon had listed all her afterschool plans for the term.

Rrrrrring!

"Hello, Babysitters Club," Claudia said. "Uh-huh . . . Okay, Dr Johanssen, I'll call you back in a second." *Click!* "Saturday, three to five?"

"Um, you're free, Stacey," Mary Anne replied.

"Fine," Stacey said.

The phone rang again before Claudia could reach for the receiver. "Hello, Babysitters Club."

The meeting went on like that for almost the whole half hour. It wasn't until 5:49 that I asked, "Any new business?"

"Yes," Claudia said. "I move we get me a phone with a headset or something. My arm's tired."

"I move we ask Shannon to be a regular," Stacey suggested. "We need her."

"I thought she was coming today," Mary Anne remarked.

"She rang me and said she couldn't make it," I informed them. "Today was

28

the first meeting of the astronomy club."

"*Astronomy?*" Mallory said.

"Otherwise known as the space cadets," Claud replied, popping a Milk Bottle in her mouth.

"Er, I hate to say this, but I don't think she'll be able to take Dawn's place," I announced.

"That's a shame," Stacey murmured.

"What about Logan?" Jessi asked.

Mary Anne shook her head. "He has football practice every day. But he said he'd try to take a few more weekend jobs."

"Uh-oh!" Claudia chanted in a robotlike voice: "Warning. Warning. Babysitting overload. Please send cloning equipment."

"Hey," I said, "we've been in this situation before. We were fine."

"Yes, but we were fine because of Shannon," Jessi said.

"Shannon will still *sit*," I reminded her. "She just can't attend meetings."

"So we're still a full member short," Stacey said.

"We could turn down a job or two if we have to," Mallory suggested. "There's no law against that."

I glared at her.

"Oops," she squeaked. "Maybe there is."

29

The room fell silent for a moment. Finally Mary Anne said, "What about finding a new member, Kristy?"

I knew someone would suggest that.

Just the thought of it made me dizzy and a little sick. Our last few attempts to take on new members had been total disasters. The Babysitters Club could not afford to have a dud. It could ruin our reputation.

"Let me think about it," I said.

Rrrrrring!

"Hello, Babysitters Club," Stacey said. "Saturday? I'll check and call back."

Gulp!

Stacey gave me an impish smile and sang, "I hope you're thinking fa-ast!"

3rd CHAPTER

On Wednesday night I dreamed we took an alien into the BSC. She looked normal whenever she arrived at a client's house. But when the parents left, her skin would glow green and she'd take the kids for rides on her spaceship.

The kids loved it. The parents never suspected a thing. Neither did the BSC, until the new member started firing lasers at Claudia's bedroom.

I woke up shivering.

Dreams are supposed to reflect your deepest fears. Was I, Kristy Thomas, born leader and decision-maker, afraid of the idea of a new BSC member?

You bet!

When Stacey brought up the subject during our Friday meeting, I told her I was still thinking.

31

Well, I was, but it wasn't the only thing on my mind. The Krushers were another. Our practice that afternoon had been atrocious. The World Series was to begin the next day, and the kids were super-nervous and not concentrating. At one point Jake Kuhn swung his bat too hard and somehow hit himself on the head. Jackie Rodowsky collided with Matt Braddock and gave him a swollen lip. Nina Marshall managed to walk off with third base while no one was looking and lost it somewhere. (Yes, lost the base.) Then one of our old softballs fell apart, and David Michael spent most of the practice pulling out the stuffing.

You know what the worst part was? Bart stopped by towards the end of practice. He watched for a while and said, "We could postpone it for a week."

I don't even want to tell you what I said.

The third thing on my mind was the mystery of my new neighbours. I thought the family would have moved in by the first day of school, but they hadn't. If they had been in the house, I would have seen them.

They didn't turn up on the second day either, or the third. Each day on the way to school and on the way home, I looked at the house they were supposed to move into. The building workers' lorries were still in the drive, but no mini-van or estate car. (I don't know why I assumed they'd have a mini-van or estate car. I just did.)

By Friday I was starting to worry. But I decided they must have been delayed for a week, maybe because of one of the parents' jobs. So I vowed to keep my eye open for the new family all weekend.

Believe it or not, I felt rather angry. Where were they? Who did they think they were, making me run over to their house in vain all the time? With all I had to think about?

I know. I was being ridiculous. Still, you have to admit, it was pretty weird. I mean, as far as I know, parents do not love keeping their kids out of school unless it's absolutely necessary.

I could understand it if the house were a mess. But it wasn't. It looked pretty good. Beautiful, really. The workers had put in a dark, carved-wood front door. They'd also added a huge porch with a swing, as well as a chimney and a U-shaped drive and new wood shingles and a small side extension with a bay window.

In comparison, Mrs Porter's house (the one between ours and the phantom family's) was looking worse and worse.

To begin with, it's a dark, old, run-down Victorian house. You expect tortured howling to come out of the attic gable windows at night. Mrs Porter herself looks like a witch. I'm not saying this to be unkind. It's simply true. Her hair is grey and frizzy, the tip of her nose has a wart, and she always dresses in black. My stepsister, Karen, calls her Morbidda Destiny. (Karen's *convinced* she's a witch.)

I was suddenly afraid the family had taken one look at what was next door and fled.

Sorry. Mrs Porter is a very nice person. I was just in a mood.

On the way home from the Friday BSC meeting, I noticed Miss Steinert on the lawn of the mystery twins' house.

When Charlie had parked in our drive, I climbed out of the car and walked over to her. She was concentrating on her clipboard.

"Hi!" I called out.

She looked up for a moment. "Oh, hello, dear." She looked down.

"Still working?" I asked. (I know, but I had to start somewhere.)

Miss Steinert rolled her eyes. "Oh, yes. Until we make it perfect."

"Looks great to me."

"To me, too. And to the workers."

Miss Steinert sighed. "But not, I'm afraid, to your future neighbours."

"What's wrong?"

"Oh, the kitchen wallpaper, the toilet seats, the colour of the living room carpet, the size of the hall mirror, the design of the newel posts—"

"You mean, they've been here to see it?"

"On Wednesday, at about five-thirty. The mother told me the house has to be completely finished before they move in, to avoid too much upheaval with her daughters." Miss Steinert shrugged. "I suppose starting the girls in their old school and then taking them out after a couple of weeks is less of an upheaval. . ."

Her voice trailed off. She seemed embarrassed. I don't think she meant to talk about her client like that. Then she excused herself and hurried into the house.

I suppose I wasn't the only person with a lot on her mind.

I walked home. In the kitchen, Sam was making iced tea, Charlie was mopping up a spill, David Michael was looking sheepish, and Watson was busy squeezing lemons over a cold bluefish salad with dill and tarragon. (Does that sound awful? It's not. Watson is a great cook.)

I gathered up cutlery and plates. As I was laying the table for dinner, the door-bell rang.

"I'll get it!" I called.

I ran to the door and pulled it open. I almost gasped.

Morbidda Destiny was staring me in the face.

"Hi, Mor—Mrs Porter," I said.

"Hello, Kristy," she cackled (that is the only word to describe that voice). "I was wondering if I might have a word with your parents."

Uh-oh! I didn't like the sound of this. A vision popped into my head. She had kidnapped the mystery neighbours and put them in a witch's brew. Now she felt guilty and wanted to confess to someone.

I ran into the kitchen and told Mum and Watson who was at the door.

They gave each other a curious look. "You and your brothers can finish laying the table, then help Nannie with your sister until we're ready."

"Okay."

Very calmly, without the slightest fear, they wiped their hands, poured out three glasses of iced tea, and walked into the living room.

Helping Nannie with Emily Michelle was harder than it sounded. Emily needed

36

a clean nappy. She is in an *I hate nappy changes* phase. We had to chase her around the whole of the ground floor.

Charlie finally cornered her and tickled her all the way to the changing table. I helped Sam and David Michael bring things out to the dining room, but mostly I hung around within earshot of the living room.

". . . all a shock to me," I heard Mrs Porter saying. "I thought their marriage was solid as a rock. My daughter has custody, but she wants to move away from Stoneybrook. My granddaughter doesn't say much about it, but I can tell she's very upset."

My heart sank. I knew Mrs Porter's granddaughter. Her name is Dru (short for Druscilla). She's seven and she used to play with Karen. When Dru's parents were first looking for a house in Stoneybrook, Dru had stayed with Mrs Porter for a while.

I absolutely hate hearing about divorces. Poor kid.

"How awful," my mum remarked. "Will she and your daughter stay in the house?"

"Well, no. My daughter doesn't want to live anywhere near Stoneybrook. In fact, she's already found a buyer for the house, and she's looking for a job and a flat elsewhere." Mrs Porter sighed. "She wants Dru to live with me while she does this. She feels Dru will be more secure if she continues in her class at Stoneybrook Day School."

The room fell silent.

Clink! Clank! Bang! I let the cutlery clatter as I laid the table, to make myself sound busy.

"Your children have been through separation and divorce," Mrs Porter continued. "What shall I do? What kinds of behaviour should I expect from Druscilla? How can I make her feel better about this mess? I hope you don't mind my asking."

Gulp!

I wanted to take back every stupid "witch" thought I had ever had. Mrs Porter sounded as if she were going to cry.

Clinkity-clank! I rearranged the salad forks.

"Hey, when are we going to eat?" Charlie muttered, stalking into the dining room.

Sam was right behind him. "What's she doing, casting a spell?"

"Tooo-nah!" Emily Michelle shrieked from the kitchen. (She thought the bluefish was tuna salad.)

"Shhhhh!" I said.

I could hear Mum giving Mrs Porter all kinds of great advice—to be a good listener, don't ignore Dru's feelings, arrange lots of interesting activities, stuff like that.

Then Watson said, "Mrs Porter, Druscilla is welcome in our house any time. And as you know, our daughter Kristy is an extremely competent babysitter."

I smiled.

Good old Watson!

By Saturday morning, the mystery house had been painted a sand colour, and a new dogwood tree had been planted in the front garden. The builders had gone, and so had Miss Steinert.

While I was doing the breakfast dishes, I heard car doors slamming outside. Then I heard some unfamiliar female voices.

"It's them!" I cried.

"Who?" Charlie asked.

"The twins!"

"What twins?"

I ran to the living room. Then I nonchalantly walked outside, as if I just *had* to inspect the rhododendrons that very minute.

When I glanced up the street, I saw a car at the kerb. But not in front of the phantom family's house. It was in front of Mrs Porter's house. Druscilla and her mother were lifting luggage out of the boot.

Lots of luggage. Dru was obviously staying a long time.

"And the houses in Mercer have become so expensive," Dru's mum was saying, "and what with the mortgage rates and the points and banks and frabbajabba. . ."

Well, something like that. I'd kind of tuned out. I was looking at Dru's face.

She was pale. Her eyes were small and red-rimmed. Her hair, which is thick and black, was kind of messed up. A few strands were stuck wetly to her forehead.

The breath stuck in my throat. I felt tears welling up. That hardly ever happens to me. I could guess how Dru was feeling.

"Well, I'm so happy you'll be staying with me!" Mrs Porter said, holding her arms out to Druscilla.

Dru just stood there for a moment. Then she took a couple of steps forwards and let Mrs Porter hug her.

I felt funny just hanging around. I spotted a plastic straw among the flowers in our front garden, picked it up, and went inside the house.

I threw the straw away and finished the

breakfast dishes. Then I ran outside again, put some air in my bike tyres, and repaired David Michael's glove, which was falling apart.

Next I sauntered into the front garden. I looked next door. Nonchalantly.

Still no car in front of the mystery house. Mrs Porter's daughter's car had gone, too.

But Druscilla was sitting on the steps of her grandmother's house, staring into the street.

I walked towards her. "Hi!" I called.

She looked at me as if I were a cold plate of leftover asparagus. "Hi," she mumbled.

"I'm Kristy. Karen's sister."

"I know."

I sat down next to her. "Karen's staying overnight on Wednesday, and then she'll be living with us all next month."

"Good."

"She'll be so surprised to see you."
Silence.

"Happy, too," I added quickly.

"Uh-huh."

"You're in second grade?"
Nod.

"So you go to school with Melody Korman, right? She lives down the street."

"Uh-huh."

"And Hannie Papadakis lives in that house." I pointed across the street.

"I know."

"So you'll have plenty of kids to play with."

"That's only two," Dru said glumly.

"Well, two who're in second grade. Three, if you count Karen. But plenty of other kids live in the neighbourhood. Maria Kilbourne is eight. She goes to your school too, doesn't she?" Then I had an idea. "You know, a lot of kids belong to this softball team I coach. Kristy's Krushers."

Dru looked at me blankly.

"We're practising to play Bart's Bashers in our own World Series. It's really fun. Want to join us?"

Dru grimaced. "I'm useless at sports."

"Well, you'll be perfect for the team!" I blurted out. "I mean, not that everyone is useless, but a lot of the kids are just beginners. Nobody's a real expert. We play mainly for fun. You should try it. Or you could be a cheerleader. We have three of them, you know."

Dru made a face.

"Look, our first game is this afternoon," I said. "Why don't you come and watch?"

"Well, maybe," she muttered, in a way

that sounded a lot more like no than yes.

But it was a start. I could work on her.

We chatted a little more, until Mrs Porter called her inside.

I said goodbye and went home. As I walked across the lawn, Mrs Porter's house cast a jagged shadow over me. What a place to live in after your parents split up! I'd be depressed, too.

Before I went inside, I examined the mystery house. It was still empty, practically shiny with its new paint job.

Too bad Dru and her grandmother couldn't live there.

4th
CHAPTER

"*Matt! Matt! Matt! Matt! Matt!*" screamed the Krusher cheerleading squad.

Our cheerleaders are Haley Braddock and Vanessa Pike (one of Mal's sisters), who are nine years old, and Charlotte Johanssen, who's eight.

The whole of the Krusher team had joined in the cheer, along with a crowd of family, friends, BSC members and a few people who had wandered over from the pavement. (Druscilla, unfortunately, wasn't one of them.) Everyone had spread out picnic blankets on the ground where the spectators' benches used to be. But now all the food was being ignored. The game was too exciting.

It was the bottom of the last inning. The Krushers were behind, 15-12, the bases were loaded, and our best hitter was up. If Matt could manage to make it home, we'd win.

Me? I was in shock. A state of total, absolute flabbergast. (Is that a word? I hope so. It's perfect.)

I'll admit it. After Friday's practice, I expected us to be trounced. Not that I gave up hope. I didn't. But I honestly thought we'd need a game or two to build up our confidence.

I was so wrong! My little sluggers were playing to win. Even Gabbie was two for three (okay, maybe the pitcher let her reach base one time).

Matt Braddock cocked his bat. He stared intently at the Basher pitcher. We knew he couldn't hear us cheering (Matt was born profoundly deaf, and he communicates with American Sign Language, or ASL), but we also knew he felt our energy.

"Matt! Matt! Matt! Matt! Matt!"

The pitcher threw the ball. Matt swung and missed.

"Strike one!" called Watson, who was umpiring.

"Stike one!" I could hear Emily Michelle pipe up from the sidelines.

The crowd quietened down. The catcher threw the ball back to the pitcher.

I scanned the base runners. Jackie

Rodowsky had planted his left foot on first. Margo Pike was on second. At third base, Patsy Kuhn had turned her cap back to front and was dancing dreamily with her eyes closed.

"Look alive, runners!" I called out.

Crrrrack!

I had missed seeing the pitch. But I saw the ball bounce towards second base. The Basher shortstop and second base player ran for it. Either one could have caught it.

But neither of them called for the ball. Instead, they collided. The ball skipped past them into right field.

Matt's face could have lit up the Astrodome.

"Go! Go! Go!" I called out, waving them all on.

Patsy skipped home. Margo charged around third and *slid* home, even though the ball was still bouncing harmlessly in the outfield. Jackie, who had decided to watch the ball's journey, started running late. Matt ended up chasing him around the basepaths.

When Matt stepped on home plate, I yelled so loudly I think I pulled a neck muscle. I ran to Matt and lifted him in the air. Around us, the crowd was storming on to the field.

We had won, 16-15.

We led the series, one game to none!

You should have seen the Krushers. I let go of Matt and then Linny, Buddy, Margo, Jake and Hannie picked him up and paraded him around. Matt was laughing like crazy. David Michael, Patsy, Laurel, and Jamie were doing a funny victory dance.

"Kristyyyyyy!" Karen and Andrew threw their arms around me and started jumping up and down.

Bart was in a state of shock. I could tell, because he was standing with his hands in his pockets, looking loose and carefree. He never looks like that unless he loses.

Now, I am not putting Bart down. I am a good sport. It doesn't make me happy that he lost. (But, I admit, it would have made me a lot less happy if he'd won.)

"Okay, everyone, let's do the Basher cheer!" I shouted.

The Krushers gathered around me. When they were all paying attention, I led the chanting: "Two, four, six, eight! Who do we appreciate? The Bashers! The Bashers! Yeeaaaa!"

On the other side of the diamond, the Bashers returned the cheer. Then Bart and I led the players to the pitcher's mound, where they lined up for high-fives. (Isn't that a great tradition? I believe all players should be good sports, win or lose.)

Both teams rushed to the sidelines, tearing into the food supply. Left and right, kids were re-enacting game highlights, even some I didn't remember.

As I walked towards my mum, my hand was getting sore from giving high-fives.

"Congratulations, Coach!" Mum said, handing me a sandwich.

"Thanks." I was so hungry! I wolfed it down, then grabbed another.

"Very nice game," an unfamiliar voice said behind me.

My mouth was full of peanut butter and bread. I had a tuna sandwich in my right hand, a juice carton in my left. I turned to face a heavily built, balding man wearing Bermuda shorts and a T-shirt that said *Natt's Nappies*.

"Fonx." I should never talk with my mouth full. I meant to say "Thanks." I also meant to keep my food inside my mouth. Instead, I sent a small piece of bread hurtling past the guy's left elbow.

Luckily, he did not seem to notice. "Neil Natt," he said, offering his hand. "Of Natt's Nappies."

I swallowed. "The nappy service! I remember. You used to bring nappies for my brother, before Mum switched to disposables." Oops! I have such a big mouth. I quickly added, "I mean, that was when he was almost old enough to stop wearing them. She always believed terry nappies were better for the environment." (I didn't mention that Emily Michelle used disposable nappies exclusively.)

Mr Natt chuckled. "She's right. Very few companies like ours exist any more. We're one of the brave holdouts. It takes guts to hang on to something you believe in. Stick-to-it-iveness! Spirit! Which, I might add, are the qualities your team has."

"Thanks, Mr Natt," I said. The smell of popcorn was wafting towards me and I really wanted some.

But Mr Natt barged on. "I couldn't help noticing how worn-out your equipment is. Not to mention your . . . uniforms. I was wondering if your team has a sponsor?"

"No, we're really just an informal kind of—"

"Well, I may be able to help you. You need funds, and I need an effective way to advertise. I just happened to be walking past the field, and I saw how many young families were watching. Families with babies and toddlers. And every time I see babies, I think Natt's Nappies. That was when the idea hit me. I could provide your team with spanking-new uniforms and equipment. Your kids will feel good about themselves, and their parents will be proud. At the same time, they'll think of Natt's Nappies. What a great opportunity for us both!"

It didn't sound like a bad idea. Actually, I was pretty impressed. Good advertising ideas are hard to dream up. I should know. I spend a lot of time trying to think of them for the BSC. And the Krushers did need the equipment.

Still, I didn't want to jump into the decision. My mind was on the game. I wanted to celebrate the victory with my team. And besides, I wasn't sure I liked the idea of sponsorship. It sounded so official.

"Can I think about it?" I asked.

Mr Natt smiled and handed me his business card. "Of course. Call me when you make a decision."

My mum is great. She insisted on taking the whole team (and friends and families) out for ice cream after the game. What a crowd! When we walked into the Rosebud Cafe, I thought the staff were going to faint.

All the kids squeezed around several tables near the back. Most of the adults stood and chatted.

That was when I brought up Mr Natt's idea to my parents. I mentioned the things Mr Natt had promised. As I did, I became more and more excited.

At last Watson said, "So, what's the downside?"

"Well, the Krushers might feel a little too ... I don't know, formal or something," I replied. "It might not be as much fun."

Mum laughed. "Kids love uniforms, Kristy. They'll think they've been transformed into pros."

"I say go for it," Watson added.

Two for, none against, one undecided.

I decided to bring it up before the world's biggest Krushers fans, the BSC.

Monday's meeting was another killer. The phone rang so much, I didn't have a chance to mention my dilemma until almost six o'clock.

Mallory and Stacey thought sponsorship was a great idea.

Claudia said, "I think you should have some kind of veto power over the costumes."

"Uniforms," I corrected her.

"Whatever," Claudia replied. "I mean,

what if they're ugly? Or orange or some-thing. You don't want the kids to be traumatized."

I burst out laughing. "Claudia Kishi, sports fashion consultant."

"What's the team going to be called?" Jessi asked. "Natt's Krushers?"

"Kristy's Nappies," Mallory said.

"Kristy's Krushed Nappies?" Claudia suggested.

The room exploded with laughter. I threw a crumpled-up Snickers wrapper at Claudia.

At last Mary Anne said, "What if he does want to change the team name?"

"I don't know," I said.

"No 'Kristy' on the uniform?" Claudia said. "You'd hate it!"

"Not true!" I shot back. "I want what-ever's best for the kids."

Stacey nodded. "Then you have one choice, really. I think you should do it."

"Me, too," Jessi agreed.

It was unanimous.

At home, after the meeting, I called Mr Natt. I reached him just as he was shutting up shop.

"So what's the decision, Coach Thomas?" he asked.

"The answer is yes," I replied.

"Terrific," he said with a laugh. "Send me your sizes straight away, and you'll have team uniforms in a week."

5th CHAPTER

Tuesday

Guys, it felt so good to babysit this afternoon. I mean it. It seems like forever since my last job.

Anyway, I think I managed to make friends with Druscilla. I'm not sure, though. With her, it's kind of hard to tell.

I don't know why Shannon was complaining. We'd offered her lots of jobs. But for a week and a half, she had turned them all down.

Why? I'll tell you. Shannon was starstruck. And stagestruck. She had been elected vice-chairman of the astronomy club and been chosen to play one of the leading roles in a drama club production of *Arsenic and Old Lace*.

She was thinking of joining the Spanish club, too.

Shannon's life was one big club sandwich. And the Babysitters Club was just one of the ingredients, like a withered piece of iceberg lettuce slipping out the side.

(Sorry. I don't mean to sound bitter. It's just that I hadn't expected Shannon to give us *less* time than before.)

Okay, enough complaining. Back to the Saga of Druscilla.

I had prepared Shannon at the Monday BSC meeting. I had told her how sad Dru was. I'd explained about the forthcoming divorce. Shannon's eyes had grown misty. She said she understood. (Her family life hasn't been running smoothly recently. She worries all the time about her parents' marriage.)

Shannon brought a fully stocked

Kid-Kit to her job. Mrs Porter met her at the door.

"Thank you for coming, Shannon," she said. "I'll be at the optician's for an hour or so, and then I have to do my marketing. I'll be back before supper. Druscilla is in the study."

(Mrs Porter is the only person I know who calls shopping "marketing".)

When Mrs Porter had left, Shannon walked through the house and into the study.

Druscilla was lying on the sofa. On her chest, she held open an old photo album. All the photos were black-and-white.

"Hi!" Shannon said. "I'm Shannon Kilbourne."

Dru didn't look up. "Hi," she muttered.

"What are you looking at?"

"An album."

"Those look like old pictures."

"Yes."

Shannon knelt down next to her and peered at a pregnant, smiling woman in a long coat. A huge bridge was in the background.

"Is that your grandmother?" Shannon asked.

"Yes. She lived in Brooklyn. That's in New York City." She placed her finger on Mrs Porter's protruding belly. "That's my mum in there."

"Wow! She was beautiful."

Dru gave her a look. "How can you tell? She wasn't even born."

Shannon laughed. "I mean your grandmother."

Dru began leafing through the rest of the album. Shannon watched Mrs Porter grow into Morbidda Destiny. She saw Dru's mum take her first steps, spill spaghetti on her head, ride a bike, go to a high school dance and graduate from college.

The moment Dru turned to wedding pictures, she closed the book.

"I'm bored," she announced.

Shannon felt a knot in her stomach. Poor Dru didn't want to see her mum and dad all happy and young and full of hope.

"I've brought a colouring book," Shannon said, opening her Kid-Kit. "With watercolour pencils."

"No, thanks."

"Okay. Want to play catch with this mini-Frisbee?"

"No."

"Have you ever read *Esio Trot* or *Tiffky Doofky*? I've brought those."

"I've read them."

"Monopoly Junior?"

Dru turned over and looked at the Kid-

Kit. "Did you fit all of that in there?"

Aha, a flicker of interest! "Yes. Do you know how to play?"

"Yes. But I don't want to just now."

"What would you like to do?"

"Nothing."

Dru plopped back on the sofa again.

Being an excellent babysitter (even if she does belong to too many clubs), Shannon knew just what to do. "No problem," she said. "I'll be in the kitchen if you change your mind."

I hate to give away trade secrets, but that always works. With Dru, it took about three minutes.

She slumped into the kitchen and gave a huge sigh. Then she sat opposite Shannon and put her head on the table, nestled in her arms.

"Are you tired?" Shannon asked.

"No," Dru mumbled.

"Just sad?"

Dru shrugged.

"You know, if you want to talk about it, it's okay."

Dru's face began to go red. She looked as if she would either scream or cry.

"I don't *have* to," she blurted out.

"Of course you don't. I was just—"

"Now I'm talking. Okay? If you want to hear more talking, turn on the TV."

"Dru?"

"Talk, talk, talk. You and my mum and my grandma always ask me to *talk*. Why is talking so great? *I hate talking!*"

Now tears were rolling down Dru's cheeks. Shannon gently put her hand on Dru's arm, but Dru pulled it away.

"I'm sorry," Shannon said. "I didn't mean to upset you."

She spotted a box of tissues on the worktop and brought them to Dru. Then she helped Dru wipe her tears.

For a long while, neither of them said a word. Dru just stared into the distance. She looked as if she'd forgotten Shannon was there. At last she took a deep breath and said, "My grandma makes awful sandwiches. She uses this mushy bread, and orange marmalade. It's so pukey."

Shannon wasn't expecting that. But she nodded and replied, "I know what you mean. Whenever my dad makes jam sandwiches, he uses too much jam, and presses really hard when he cuts it so the jam oozes through."

"And when you pick it up, it feels so yucky," Dru remarked.

"Like a wet sponge."

"Like slugs!"

"Ugh!"

Druscilla was smiling now. "I hate slugs!"

"Me, too!"

"I used to take the salt cellar outside and pour salt on them," Dru said, her eyes lighting up.

"Ugh! And you watched them shrivel up?"

"Dad used to get so angry with me. . ."

Dru's voice trailed off.

Yikes! Shannon could see the light starting to go off inside Dru. Quickly she said, "You know, it's really nice outside. Let's go for a walk. I can show you my house, and maybe we can visit some kids you know in the neighbourhood."

To Shannon's surprise, Dru nodded and stood up.

Shannon wrote a note to Mrs Porter explaining what she and Dru were doing. Then the girls walked out of the back door and down the drive. "That was stupid," Dru said, almost whispering.

"What was?" Shannon asked.

"Pouring salt on the slugs. I should never have done that." Dru looked as if she were going to cry again. "I knew Dad didn't like it. He told me and told me."

"Listen, kids do things like that. Are you worried that's why your dad and mum . . . you know?"

"Maybe if I wasn't so stupid all the time—"

Shannon put her arm around Dru. This time Dru didn't move away. "Dru, it wasn't your fault."

Dru didn't answer. But on the way to the Kilbournes', her arm was tight around Shannon's waist.

Maria, Shannon's eight-year-old sister, ran to the door. "Hi!" she said. "You're Drizzelda aren't you? In Melody's grade?"

Shannon wanted to kick her.

"Druscilla," Dru replied.

"We were just going for a walk," Shannon said. "Want to join us?"

"Not now. I'm playing Boggle with Tiffany. I beat her last time."

"You did not!" Tiffany's voice bellowed from inside.

"Don't listen to her, Druscilla. Anyway, I'm glad you've moved here. We'll play, okay?"

"Okay," Dru replied.

Next stop on the tour was the Hsus' house. Timmy Hsu is six and Scott Hsu is seven, and they go to Dru's school, Stoneybrook Day.

"What are *you* doing here?" was Scott's greeting. (He wasn't being rude, just curious.)

Dru shrugged. "Living with my grandma."

"Are your parents divorced or dead or something?" Timmy asked.

Needless to say, Shannon and Dru did not stay there long.

They doubled back along McLelland Street. They walked past the House of the Phantom Twins (yes, it was still empty, but for the last couple of days Miss Steinert had been helping unload furniture deliveries from department-store vans). Then they visited the Papadakises to say hello to Hannie.

She was thrilled to see Druscilla. Mrs Papadakis allowed her to join Shannon's tour. The caravan travelled on to the Kormans', home of Melody Korman, another seven-year-old in Dru's class.

"Mum, I have to play with Dru!" was the first thing Melody said after she opened the front door.

Minutes later, the four girls were strolling to Stoneybrook playground. Dru, Hannie and Melody chatted all the way.

"We have so much fun in this neighbourhood," Melody said to Dru. "You'll love it. We have lots of parties and games—"

"Krushers is the best part," Hannie cut in.

"It is not," Melody retorted. "Just because you belong to it."

"You should, too," Hannie said. "You and Dru. I'll help you learn to play."

Melody sighed. "You always say that."

They'd reached the playground. The girls ran to the swings. For the first time that day, Dru didn't look miserable. Shannon was relieved.

6th CHAPTER

"Ahhhh-choo!"

Have you ever seen a phantom with allergies? Well, one of them moved into my neighbourhood that Wednesday. Together with two non-sneezing phantoms. One looks just like the sneezer and the other was obviously their mother.

Yes, that's right. The Phantom Phamily was here.

I couldn't believe my eyes.

And guess what they arrived in? A mini-van! Well, not in just a mini-van. A medium-sized removal van, too.

"Sir? Sir? That is a vase, not a football!" the mother phantom instructed the removal men. "And the long piece is extremely fragile. How would you carry a newborn baby? And don't say over your shoulders!"

The mum winked at her daughters. They were cracking up. The removal men were trying to keep a straight face. I was, too.

Charlie and I had seen the van on the way home from the BSC meeting. This time, even he was curious. We pulled up to the kerb, climbed out, and watched.

We weren't the only ones. The entire Papadakis family was walking towards us from across the street. Mr Papadakis was holding a foil-covered dish and smiling proudly.

"Krush-*ers*! Krush-*ers*! Krush-*ers*!" Linny and Hannie started chanting.

Soon Dru and Karen wandered over from my house (Karen and Andrew were staying the night because their mother and stepfather, the Engels, had to stay overnight in New York City). A few other neighbours stopped by, too. The mother phantom soon fell into a conversation with Mrs Korman.

The twins, however, were all business. They were bustling around, climbing in and out of the van, running into the house every few seconds.

What did they look like? Well, identical, of course. Identically glamorous, too, was my first impression. They were well dressed and deeply tanned, and they seemed older than twelve or thirteen. Why? Probably because of their height (at least five-foot seven or so), but also because of the way they acted. Even while their mum was chatting, they were in motion, confidently telling the removal men (and each other) what to do. They looked as if they'd moved a hundred times already.

Their hair and eyes were the deepest brown, almost black. But they weren't hard to tell apart. The one with allergies wore glasses and had long, thick hair, so curly it was almost in ringlets. She was wearing baggy tartan shorts and a U4Me T-shirt. (Bad sign. I cannot stand U4Me's music.) The other twin had no glasses. Her hair was shorter, and she had a fringe. She was wearing khaki trousers, sandals and a short-sleeved button-down shirt.

They were obviously busy. I didn't want to interrupt. But I didn't want to stand there looking stupid, either.

"Hi!" I said to the nearest twin (the short-haired, trousered, non-sneezing one). "I'm Kristy Thomas."

"Hi, Kristy!" She smiled and put out her hand. "I'm Anna Stevenson."

"Hello," said the other. "I'b Abby. You live id this deighbourhood?"

(Guess which one had the allergies?)

"Two houses down," I said. "Need some help?"

"Yes!" said Abby. "Wadda swab siduses?"

I looked at her blankly. "Huh?"

"Devver bide." Laughing to herself, she picked up a suitcase and walked towards the house. "I'll go ad fide a decodgesdud."

"Don't mind her," Anna said. "She's just being Abby. Her sense of humour grows on you."

I don't know why I started thinking of fungus.

"And thanks for the offer, but don't worry about helping," Anna added. "All the heavy stuff is here already. Mum ordered it directly from the shops."

A house full of brand-new furniture? Either they were completely loaded, or their old stuff was hideous. I didn't exactly want to ask which.

"My best friend's boyfriend's little brother, Hunter Bruno, is allergic to everything," I said, watching Abby disappear into the house.

"Does he have asthma, too?" Anna asked. "Abby does. Maybe they should meet."

"Hunter's five," I replied.

"Oops!" Anna laughed.

"Welcome!" Mr Papadakis thundered, walking over to us. As he handed Anna the foil-covered dish, a familiar car pulled up to the kerb.

Miss Steinert climbed out. She did not look too happy. "What—why—" she stammered, walking towards Mrs Stevenson. "You're here!"

"Hello, Sylvia," Mrs Stevenson said. "The place looks spectacular."

"Thanks," Miss Steinert replied, "but—well, today is Wednesday. You said you were arriving tomorrow."

"I changed our plans last week. Didn't my assistant phone your office?"

"No."

Mrs Stevenson rolled her eyes. "My apologies. I thought I had the whole week off, but my boss arranged an editorial meeting for Friday. So I thought we'd move things forward a day—you know, have a full day in the new house, settle in—"

"Excuse me!" one of the movers shouted from the open door. "Nothing's on in here."

Mrs Stevenson turned. Miss Steinert looked pale.

"I beg your pardon?" Mrs Stevenson replied.

"No juice," the man said. "Nothing."

Mrs Stevenson looked confused. "Well, I suppose I could run over to the grocer's."

"He means electricity, Rachel," Miss Steinert said. "All the services are booked to be turned on tomorrow. Phones, electricity, water, gas. You won't have any of it until then."

"Oh, dear." Mrs Stevenson looked deadly serious. "Well, we can't very well go all the way back to Long Island now."

"We've got torches," Anna said. "We'll be fine."

A hoot of laughter made us turn around. Abby was running out of the front door. "It's like the *Liddle House od the Prairie*," she said. "I love it. We'll be piodeers!"

"Er, let's not get carried away, girls," Mrs Stevenson said. "We are talking about a dark, unfamiliar house, not Yosemite Park. I'll call a hotel."

"With what phode?" Abby asked.

"Use my car phone," Miss Steinert suggested. "Call the George Washington. If they're booked, try the Strathmoore or the Sleepy Bear. I need to check some things inside. Would you like me to take the dish in, Anna?"

"All right."

The Papadakis's dish in hand, Miss

Steinert walked briskly into the house. Mrs Stevenson went over to the car phone.

A horn tooted lightly behind us. We turned to see my mum's car pull up in front of the van.

"Welcome!" Mum said to the twins as she climbed out of the car. "We thought you would never come."

Abby and Anna introduced themselves and explained what had happened.

Mum hardly waited for them to finish. "Well, then, you'll stay with us overnight, of course."

"Cool!" Abby said.

"That's so nice," Anna agreed. "Mum?"

Mrs Stevenson poked her head out of the car window. Mum introduced herself, and made the offer.

You know how grown-ups are. Mrs Stevenson refused. Mum insisted. Mrs Stevenson refused. Mum insisted.

Guess who won? (Hint: my forceful personality was inherited.)

We raced to prepare dinner. By 7:43, the house was ready. Tomato sauce was simmering on the stove. Two trays of breaded clams were baking in the oven. My mouth was watering. My brothers and I had put

70

two extra places at the dining room table, and it was now laid for thirteen.

Ding-dong! Our doorbell rang at 7:45.

"I'll get it!" I shouted.

"Rawf! Rawf!" barked Shannon (the puppy, not the human).

She was the first to reach the door. The rest of the Brewer/Thomas herd followed in approximately this order—me, Mum, Watson, my brothers, Karen, Andrew, Nannie and Emily Michelle.

I yanked the door open. "Hi!"

"*Aaaaa-choo!*" was Abby's response.

"Bless you!" Watson said. "Come on in."

The Stevensons stepped into the living room. Anna was holding the dish Mr Papadakis had given them, and Abby and her mum carried overnight bags. I noticed Abby wasn't wearing her glasses. I hoped she hadn't sneezed them off.

"I don't know how I can begin to thank you—" Mrs Stevenson began.

"Rawf! Rawf!" Shannon jumped on Abby, wagging her tail.

"Down, girl!" David Michael ordered, grabbing Shannon by the collar.

"YEEEEEAAA-CHOOOOO!" Abby sneezed.

"That's some cold," Mum remarked.

"It's dot," Abby replied, sniffling.

"She's allergic," Anna explained. "To dogs and dust and certain foods."

"Goodness," Mum said. "David Michael, put Shannon out the back. Sam and Charlie, take the dish into the kitchen and the bags into the guest rooms."

The boys obeyed. (They were on their best behaviour.) "Abby's allergies aren't usually so bad," Anna explained. "They're worse during times of stress and hay fever season."

"Allergies, asthba, I'b a bess!" Abby said, rubbing her eyes.

"I don't know why you put in your contact lenses," Anna murmured, as Mum led everyone into the house.

"The sabe reason *you* did," Abby retorted.

Before an argument could start, Mrs Stevenson exclaimed, "What a lovely house!"

"Daddy's a millionaire," Andrew said.

Karen poked him in the ribs with her elbow. "Ssshh!"

"Ow!" Andrew exclaimed. "What'd you do that for? He *is*."

The rest of us politely ignored him. As Mum took the Stevensons from room to room, my brothers joined us. Soon all

72

twelve of us were moving through the house together, like a herd of cattle.

Abby was having a rough time. She tried not to complain. But she sneezed again in the kitchen, and then even louder in the study.

When we showed her the room she'd be staying in, she sneezed so loudly I thought her head would fly off.

We quickly retreated to the landing. "We have a cat," Nannie said. "Could that be it?"

"Doe," Abby replied. "I'b dot allergic to cats, just cat litter."

"Then stay out of the bathroom at the end of the hall," I suggested. "That's where we keep the—"

"Aaaa-choooo!" Abby smiled. "See? Eved the thought of it gets me goig."

The caravan moved on. I ducked back into the guest bedroom and ran my fingers along the top of a chest of drawers. Dust galore.

Quietly I mentioned this to Sam and Charlie. As Mum continued the tour, we went to work. Charlie and I removed the guest room curtains and then dusted. Sam rolled up the rug, took it to the attic, then vacuumed.

By the time we had finished, the room was dust-free and ready to go.

"Dinner's ready!" Watson called from downstairs.

"Dinna wehhhd!" Emily Michelle echoed.

We bolted downstairs. Actually, dinner was *almost* ready. I helped Mum prepare the last couple of portions of the pasta. "Leave one without sauce," Mum said softly. "Mrs Stevenson told me Abby's allergic to tomatoes. She likes soy sauce and olive oil. On the side."

Yuck! I nearly choked. But I didn't. Obediently I took the ingredients out of the refrigerator and served Abby.

As we sat chatting away, Watson swept in with two steaming trays. "Clams à la Watson!" he announced, pronouncing his name *WatSONE*, in a daft French accent. "Speciality of the house."

"Ugh!" Andrew cried.

"Yummm!" said almost everyone else.

Abby's tan took on a greenish tinge.

"Are you okay?" I asked.

"Fide," she said with a tight smile.

"What other foods are you allergic to, dear?" Nannie asked.

"Shellfish," Abby replied, and she excused herself from the table.

"The sight of them makes her a little queasy," Anna explained softly.

*   *   *

Well, the clams were quickly hidden away in the fridge. Abby returned and continued dinner.

We talked about school, the BSC and Stoneybrook. The Stevensons told us about the town in Long Island where they had lived. Abby's voice slowly began to clear up. She did an imitation of her middle school head, who spoke with a posh accent, had a huge pot belly, and twisted his hair into knots whenever he spoke. That was funny.

But then she continued. She imitated three teachers. And a couple of students. And a neighbour who spoke like Daffy Duck.

Everyone was cracking up. Me? Well, I hadn't exactly expected the Abby Stevenson comedy hour. I couldn't get a word in edgewise.

At one point, David Michael asked, "When's your dad coming?"

Anna took a deep breath. "Well, he died," she replied matter-of-factly. "When we were nine."

That kind of hung in the air a moment. No one knew what to say.

"I'm sorry," Mum finally said in a gentle voice.

"How did he die?" David Michael pressed on.

I could tell Sam was giving him a kick.

"We don't have to—" Watson began.

"It's okay," Abby said. "It was a car accident."

"Ohhhh," I said. (I mean to say something sympathetic, but it came out as a groan.)

Mrs Stevenson spoke up. "The last few years have been a struggle, as you can imagine. But life goes on. I was recently made executive editor of a publishing house in New York, which was a wonderful opportunity, but it's made our lives absolutely insane. My girls have been fabulous, thank goodness. They do so much work. . ."

We chatted on. After dinner the twelve-and-over set moved into the living room for dessert (pastries from the Papadakises) while the kids wolfed down ice cream in the kitchen.

Anna went over to the piano. "Wow, a grand! Is it a Steinway?"

"Looks like a piano to me," Abby replied.

"Ha ha," Anna said under her breath.

"Yes, it is," Watson said. "Do you play?"

Anna went red. "A little. Violin is my main instrument."

"Play the Grieg piece for us," Mrs

Stevenson said. "You do that so well."

"Oh, okay," Anna said with a sigh, sitting down.

I could not believe my ears. The "Grieg piece" was fantastic. Even the kids filed in to listen. I was so impressed, I led a "two-four-six-eight" cheer for her.

Anna laughed. "You lot are sweet," she said.

I liked Anna a lot. After the concert, we sat together and talked non-stop. Well, *I* talked. I couldn't help it. Anna kept asking me questions about school, the BSC, the Krushers. She seemed genuinely interested in everything.

Not Abby, though. The moment she wasn't the centre of attention, forget it. She just wandered off without a word. Moments later I saw her and the kids in a pile on the floor, giggling hysterically.

Okay, this may sound stupid, but all I could think about was whether or not she was imitating me.

Ridiculous, I know. She wouldn't have done that right in my house.

But I kept an eye on her, anyway.

Funny how sisters can seem like people from two different planets.

7th CHAPTER

"Mu-um, where's my Batman plate?"

"The French toast is ready!"

"Yuck, I hate cinnamon!"

"My sock's got a hole!"

"Andrew's spilled his orange juice!"

"Tee-oze!"

"Nannieeeee, Emily Michelle wants Cheerios!"

"Well, go and find the sponge!"

"Hey, someone's wiped his dirty face on my towel!"

"Aaaaa-chooo!"

". . . It's sixty-six degrees, in central Stamford this morning, and we'll see a high of eighty-one today. . ."

"Who's ripped the cover off *I Am the Cheese?*"

"Teeeeez!"

At the Brewer/Thomas house, breakfast

for ten is no big sweat. When Karen and Andrew are at their parents', we're down to eight, and it's positively peaceful.

But thirteen? The place was a zoo. Absolutely out of control.

It was so much fun.

Abby came into the kitchen wearing a striped shirt and a paisley skirt. She looked shell-shocked. "What was I thinking when I packed these last night?"

Anna and I burst out laughing.

A hunk of buttered bagel flew through the air. Emily Michelle started giggling uncontrollably.

With a splat, the bagel landed on the floor (butter-side down, of course). And you know what happens to a buttery bagel on the floor, every time. . .

"Who-o-o-o-oa!" Sam was the lucky person who stepped on it. He went flying. As he landed, I saw his big toe protruding from the hole in his sock.

"Are you okay?" Mum asked.

Sam couldn't answer. He was cracking up.

As Watson cleaned up the bagel, David Michael screamed. "Look! It works!"

Before our eyes, his new green cereal bowl was turning blue. "It's magic!" he said.

(It wasn't. The bowl reacts that way to cold liquids.)

David Michael took his bowl to the sink, dumped the cereal out, and poured hot water in.

I let Mum take care of that one.

I don't remember much more of that breakfast. Just a lot of arms reaching for French toast and syrup, a couple more spills, and a trip to my bedroom to lend Abby another shirt.

Soon it was time to leave. For me, that usually meant waiting alone for the bus in front of my house. (When we moved to Watson's, my mum arranged for me to continue going to Stoneybrook Middle School, even though our house is out of the district.)

But guess where Mrs Stevenson had enrolled the twins? Yes, SMS! Neither Stoneybrook Day School nor Kelsey Middle School (which is in our district) was large enough to have an orchestra for Anna to play in.

It felt really good to have company. As we waited for the bus, Anna said, "Thanks for dust-busting our room last night. You did a great job."

"No problem," I replied. "Did you sleep all right, Abby?"

"Not bad," Abby said.

"You sound better," I remarked.

"The rrrain in Sssspain falls mmmainly on my brrrain," Abby pronounced.

I laughed. (Even though I didn't get it. Actually, a thank-you would have been just fine.)

Out of the corner of my eye, I spotted a Little League baseball skittering down the street. "Can you get that?" I heard Amanda Kerner call out.

She, Al Hall, Jacqueline Vecchio and Karl Schmauder (all Kelsey Middle School kids) were trying to play catch while walking to school.

I crouched to field the ball.

Abby darted in front of me. She scooped it off the ground, spun around, and fired the ball to Amanda.

Amanda didn't even have to move her glove to catch it. "Thanks," she said.

I closed my open jaw. "Good throw."

"My sister is sport crazy," Anna remarked.

"I am not!" Abby shot back.

"All right, all right, a *natural athlete*," Anna said. "Sorry."

I was not aware of this distinction, but they seemed to have had this discussion before.

"Want to play?" Amanda called out. "Al has an extra glove."

81

"Okay," Abby replied.

Al tossed Abby his glove. (Did anyone toss me one? Noooo.)

The ball started flying from person to person.

"Over here!" I called out, gloveless.

Not a clever move. I definitely needed a glove for Abby's throw. A bulletproof vest would have been nice, too.

"Yeeow!" I cried as the ball smacked against my hands and bounced out.

"Oops! Sorry," Abby said. "Are you okay?"

"Yes," I said through gritted teeth.

The bus trundled around the corner. Abby returned the glove, called out a "Thanks!" and grabbed her rucksack.

As we climbed on to the bus, my palms were numb. I didn't start regaining feeling in them until we were halfway to SMS.

I sat next to Anna. I thought Abby might try to squeeze into the seat next to us, but she didn't. She sat next to someone I didn't know and started chatting away.

"Do you like sport, too?" I asked Anna.

"I suppose it's okay," she replied. "But I'm not like Abby. You should see her in gym class. She's always the best, and she doesn't even try hard."

82

"I'm sort of like that, too."

"But Abby would never *dream* of actually playing on a team."

She'd rather just show off and let everybody think she's a natural, I thought.

But I kept that to myself.

"I thought you two were supposed to be identical," I said.

Anna laughed. "Sometimes it feels as if we're the same person. We can be in different places, and I'll think, *Abby needs me.* Then two seconds later the phone will ring, and it'll be Abby. It happens all the time. To her, too. But in other ways, we're like strangers. I mean, Abby would never sit and practise violin for two hours."

"Two hours?" The idea was revolting. Sort of like being stuck in a room with a screaming tomcat.

"I love the violin. Even more than the piano. I lose track of time when I'm practising. Even if it's just scales."

"I sort of feel that way about Krusher practice. Especially if the kids are paying attention."

"Uh-huh."

"The Babysitters Club, too. We have so much fun. Sometimes we laugh all the way through the meetings."

Anna nodded, smiled and looked out of the window.

"You know, the SMS orchestra is pretty good," I said.

"I hope so," Anna replied. "I'm playing for the music teacher at the beginning of the lunch break today."

"Great."

End of conversation. We both looked out of the window.

Across the aisle, Abby and four other kids were screaming with laughter.

Anna was nice. I liked her a lot. I just had to think of more things to say to her. Things she'd be interested in.

Oh, well, I suppose I'd be quiet, too, if I'd grown up with a sister like Abby.

Anna was in my maths class. Abby was in my English class, which was the period before lunch.

Abby and I walked to the canteen together, talking about our homework assignment: *What I Did Not Do This Summer, but Would Have Loved To.*

"Hobework wasd't so weird id by old school," Abby remarked. "I bead, what do you thik Bister Fiske wadts?"

I shrugged. "I think you're just supposed to use your imagination. You know, like, 'Last summer I would have loved to play with the New York Mets,' or something."

Before Abby could answer, Trevor Sandbourne and Austin Bentley raced down the corridor.

"Hi, Abby!" shouted Trevor.

"Hey, Yabby dabba doo!" shouted Austin.

"Hi!" Abby replied with a cheerful wave.

Yabby dabba doo? How did she know two of SMS's coolest guys already? And well enough to be called by a nickname?

I suppose baseball wasn't Abby's only skill.

Abby took a small bottle of nasal spray from her shoulder bag and sniffed from it. "That's better," she said. "I don't think you should write about the Mets, Kristy. That teacher seems like such a bookworm. I'd write something like, 'I wish I had read Shakespeare books and *Scarlet's Web* this summer.'"

I laughed. "*Scarlet's Web?*"

"You know. Whatever."

Claudia, Mary Anne and Stacey were already sitting at our usual table, grinning at us. (I had called them the night before and told them about the twins.)

Abby and I queued up for lunch, then sat with them.

"Everybody, this is Abby Stevenson," I said.

Abby smiled. "Hi!"

That was the last sane part of the conversation. Everyone started talking at once. Abby ended up telling her life story again.

But she didn't mind at all. In fact, she loved it. Once she got going, you couldn't stop her. She acted out the previous day's events. She imitated her mum and the removal men. She imitated Miss Steinert, gaping and stammering. And Mr Papadakis, with his huge dish. And herself when Shannon jumped on her. And Watson, with his tray of clams. (I know, I just *know*, she would have "done" me if I hadn't been there.)

Everybody was *roaring*.

The truth? She was okay, but let's just say Robin Williams has nothing to worry about.

I was glad when Anna arrived. After another round of introductions, I asked her about her orchestra audition.

"It was okay," she said.

"Are you in?" I asked.

She gave me a funny look. "Well, yes. This was more for seating. I'm going to be first violin."

"You must be pretty good," Claudia said.

"Anna wins competitions," Abby piped

up. "She even played a solo with the high school orchestra in our old town."

"Abb*yyyy*!" Anna blushed.

"She plays the piano, too," I added.

Anna was busily twirling her spaghetti and meat sauce, looking very embarrassed.

"We love music," Claudia said.

"Mostly pop and R&B," Stacey added. "Not so much heavy metal."

"My dad listens to classical at home a lot," Mary Anne said. "Did you have the EZ Lite Listening station in Long Island?"

Anna gave her a polite smile, as if she'd just swallowed a dead fly and didn't want anybody to notice. "Not that I know of."

What was so bad about EZ Lite? I didn't know a thing about it. But I did know it was time to change the subject.

We discussed Druscilla, who was starting to cheer up a little. We talked about the forthcoming World Series game (the Krushers' first as a sponsored team). We gossiped about different SMS teachers.

Lunch flew by. We invited the twins to join us after school in the front hall, where we could chat some more.

You know what the best part was? Afterwards, I didn't have the usual long, super-boring journey home alone. Now I had company. Okay, so Anna was too quiet and Abby was too loud. Still, it felt great.

8th
CHAPTER

A big box was waiting for me when I got home from school that day. On it was the Natt's Nappies logo, which looked like this:

"All *right!*" I cried.

After Saturday's game, Mr Natt had said the uniforms would arrive in a week. They were two days early.

David Michael wandered in, his mouth full of some snack. He stared at the label on the box for a moment, then said, "Does Emily Michelle get nappies in the post now?"

"These are uniforms," I said, ripping the box open.

"Emily Michelle wears uniforms?"

"No! Uniforms for the Krushers!" I reached inside and pulled out one of the shirts.

What a difference. Before this, our "uniforms" had been caps and T-shirts with the team name in iron-on letters. But this shirt was gleaming white. It was soft. It had that great, new-clothes smell.

And it had the Natt's Nappies logo printed on it.

That was it. Just two words and the drawing.

Nowhere did it say Kristy's Krushers.

Claudia's words came back to haunt me: *"No 'Kristy' on the uniform? You'd hate it!"*

She was right. Part of me wanted to stuff the shirt back in and return the box. How could I stand seeing my team wear these? How could *I* wear a uniform like this?

Kristy, you're a big girl, I chided myself. I had told Claudia I wanted what was best for the team. I had meant it, too. These were real uniforms—sturdy and professional-looking.

I vowed to keep my big mouth shut.

I turned to David Michael. He was gaping.

"Those are for us?" he asked.

"Yup," I replied. "What do you think?"

"The shirts have got *nappies* on them!"

"They're kind of. . ." I had a hard time thinking of the appropriate word, "sweet".

"What about the trousers?" David Michael asked.

I took out a pair of trousers and a cap. The logo was on both.

"Is that our name now?" David Michael asked. "The Natt's Nappies?"

"I suppose so."

David Michael looked mortified. "But I'm a Krusher! I'm not a . . . *Nappy*. I'm not!"

He stormed away.

I felt numb. For some reason, stupid radio announcements started popping into my head:

"Ladies and gentlemen, here they are, yo-o-ourrr Nappies!"

"The Nappies are trailing, folks. . ."

"And here comes the Nappy clean-up batter!"

"Now the coach is changing the pitcher's nappy—er, the Nappies' pitcher. . ."

I didn't know whether to laugh or cry.

I put the uniform back in the box and checked the living room clock. Practice was scheduled to begin in less than half an hour.

The box of uniforms was too heavy to carry by myself. Mum was still at work, and Charlie wasn't around to drive me.

I decided to borrow Emily Michelle's red truck. I ran through the house and told Nannie what I was up to. Then I went outside to the garage, loaded the equipment bag in the truck, and rolled it around to the front of the house.

David Michael was slumping across the lawn. "We're taking a kid's *truck* to practice?"

"Well, you could carry the box on your head," I said.

"Very funny."

The truck squeaked as we walked to the field. David Michael said hardly a word.

When we arrived, Bobby Gianelli was already there. So were Buddy and Suzi Barrett.

I didn't want to open the box until the whole team had arrived. So I left it, and the truck, by a tree.

Within about ten minutes, the field was swarming with players, babysitters, parents and younger siblings.

I looked around for some help. Mal was there, but she was busy putting an elastoplast on Claire's knee. Mary Anne, who was sitting for the Newtons, was feeding Jamie's baby sister, Lucy.

I was on my own. I lifted my trusty referee's whistle and blew.

Phweeeeeeet!

The field fell silent. "Okay, everyone," I said, being careful not to address them as *Krushers*. "I have some good news. We, the future champions of the World Series, will soon have all new equipment—bats, balls, a tee, even bases."

Half the team cheered. The other half gave me this *What was wrong with the old equipment?* look.

"A really nice man, who name is Mr Natt, has decided to be our team sponsor." I held the box chest-high. "These are the brand-new uniforms he sent us."

"YEEEEAAAAAAA!" No doubt about that reaction.

The team gathered around me, pushing and shoving. (Except for David Michael. He was standing, arms folded, against the backstop.)

I held my breath. I pulled out a team shirt, making sure the back was facing me.

The first face I noticed was Linny's.

He went pale. "I'm not wearing *that*!" he protested.

I turned the shirt around. This is what the front looked like:

Of course, now the back of the shirt was facing the team, complete with the drawing of the nappy.

"What's it say?" Claire asked.

"Natt's Nappies," Nicky replied.

"Dirty nappies?" Patsy said.

"Ugh!" Margo shrieked, dissolving into giggles.

Nina Marshall looked ashen. "Do we have to wear *nappies*?"

"Can we send them back?" Linny asked. "Or tell him to put 'Krushers' on them?"

"Well, no," I said. "That's his company name. The whole idea is to advertise the company."

"Why didn't you ask us first?" Jake

demanded angrily. "You always say teammates should communicate."

"Well, yes," I replied, "but I suppose . . . I don't know, I decided we needed the new stuff, that's all."

Glowering, Jake and Linny stalked away.

I felt like a fool. They were right. I should have called a team meeting and proposed the idea. The way I would have introduced a new idea in the BSC. What kind of leader was I, anyway?

I quickly found a shirt my size. "Look, everyone," I said, putting it on over my T-shirt. "I would never ask you to do something *I* didn't have to do."

For a moment, everyone sulked and grumbled. Then Jackie asked, "Kristy, can I have my uniform?"

"Do you *want* it?" Buddy said.

Jackie shrugged. "Yes. They're okay."

I found Jackie's uniform, and he put it on over his clothes. Margo, Claire, Matt, Myriah and Andrew decided to wear one or both pieces.

It was a start. I hoped the rest of the team would get used to the idea.

About ten minutes into practice, I gave up hope. The kids were so interested in the uniforms that they couldn't concentrate. They were bobbling the ball, wandering around the field, looking as if they'd run out of steam.

Mary Anne and Mal tried to help, but it was no use.

I distributed the rest of the uniforms at the end of practice, mostly to parents and carers.

Then came the long walk home with David Michael, the Great Grump of Stoneybrook.

As I turned on to our drive, he kept walking.

"Where are you going?" I asked.

"To Abby's," he snapped.

"Abby's? Why?"

"She's going to give me another pitching lesson."

"Another—?"

But he had gone.

I wheeled the truck into the garage. I stayed there for a while, until I heard Abby and David Michael's voices in the distance.

Then I crept to the fence and tried to see into the Stevensons' garden.

"Okay, now remember the signals," Abby was saying. "One finger means fast, two fingers means faster, three means recite the Boy Scout pledge—"

"Hey!" David Michael protested.

"Four fingers," Abby barged on,

"means scratch your left armpit, five means burp at the shortstop, and a closed fist means ohhhh, what a tummyache I have!"

David Michael was laughing so hard, I don't know how he managed to pitch the ball.

Abby was very funny. I have to admit that. But to joke around like that while you're teaching fundamentals?

Really, there's a time and a place for everything.

9th CHAPTER

Friday

Well, I finally met Dryscilla. And you know what? Sitting for her was not as hard as I thought it would be.

She seems smart. Pretty serious, too. But I think she keeps a lot hidden inside. I can't say I really understand her. Do you, Kristy?

"Can we go to Krushers' practice? I want to join."

Mary Anne could not believe the words were being spoken by Druscilla. She had read the entries about Dru in the BSC notebook. She had asked me for details, and I had told her everything I knew.

Mary Anne is great with shy, confused kids. She had a plan of approach for Druscilla, sort of like a flowchart.

It turned out she didn't need it.

"Well, er, are you sure?" Mary Anne asked. "The Krushers are a softball team."

"Kristy invited me," Dru said firmly. "You can phone her and ask."

"That's all right, I don't need to. I'd be happy to take you."

Mary Anne was thrilled. As they left the house, she asked Dru, "Have you got a glove?"

"No." Dru suddenly looked worried. "Should I have?"

"I don't think so," Mary Anne quickly reassured her. "I'm sure Kristy has extras."

"Are the kids really good?"

Mary Anne laughed. "No. But don't tell anyone I said so. How about you?"

"I'm rubbish."

"But I suppose you enjoy it."

Dru didn't answer. She started kicking a stone down the pavement.

At the school playground, practice was in full-swing. Actually, half-swing was more like it.

I had phoned that morning to remind each team member to wear the uniform. Out of twenty kids, only twelve did.

I was cool about it. I didn't make a big deal. I allowed them to express themselves.

But I told them if they didn't wear the uniforms to the next day's game, they couldn't play.

I know, it sounds harsh. And believe me, I still felt bad about arranging the sponsorship behind their backs. But I made sure I apologized to them. I also explained that a deal is a deal, and that I was responsible for living up to it.

I made sure I wore my own uniform, as daft as it looked.

"Okay, everyone, let's have a practice game!" (I still could not bring myself to call them the Nappies.) "The A team in the field, the B team batting."

Grumble, grumble, shuffle, shuffle.

"That's it. Way to go. Looking good. Woo, woo, woo!" (That was a cheer.) "Hey, big game tomorrow."

Ugh! I sounded pathetic.

You know who I was thinking about then? Dawn Schafer. I really wished she were there. Not that she was a great athlete or anything. She wasn't. But she had the most incredible energy. Her dad's nickname for her is Sunshine, and it suits her. She'd know how to cheer up the team. She'd say just the right things.

Me, I muddled along the best I could.

As Mary Anne and Dru approached, we were in the second inning of our game. How were we doing? Well, let's put it this way. If it were possible for both sides to lose, they would have.

I waved to Mary Anne. I assumed she and Dru were on their way somewhere else.

"Jake, play closer to the bag!" I yelled as Matt Braddock's ground ball skipped by him. (Actually, what I wanted to say was, "Wake up!" Jake hadn't even been looking at the ball.)

Next thing I knew, Mary Anne and Dru were at my side.

"Guess what? Dru wants to play," Mary Anne announced.

I couldn't believe it. I should have been thrilled, but I wasn't. Now that we were in the middle of a championship, now that half the team was on the verge of mutiny—*now* Druscilla wanted to join.

Easy, Kristy, I told myself. Don't be a grouch.

I smiled at Dru. I thought back to our conversation. She was coming out of her shell, showing an interest. I knew how important that was.

I reached into the equipment bag. "Righty or lefty?"

"Righty," Dru replied.

"Here's a glove. Have you got a position you especially like?"

Dru shrugged.

"Okay, let's try you out in short left field."

"Where's that?" Dru asked.

I pointed. "Over there, behind Buddy."

Dru walked grimly towards left field. She looked as if she were on her way to a maths exam.

She was also struggling to put her glove on her right hand.

"Other hand, Dru!" I called out cheerfully. "You catch with your left, throw with your right."

Well, she did neither. She stood grimly in left field and kind of waved at the only ball that came near her.

At her batting turn, we had to set up the tee (above age five or six, we usually use pitchers). She managed to knock the ball off, but that was about it.

I wanted to give Dru personal attention, but with twenty other gloomy players to manage, it wasn't easy. (I love Mary Anne dearly, but she was no help. She still thinks you score touchdowns in baseball.)

I have to say, Dru was not a quitter. She stuck it out to the end.

She even had a chance to play in front of Mr Natt himself.

Yes, he turned up during the last inning. I could hear his voice shouting, "Hey, Coach, nice uniforms!"

I was horrified. "Hi!" I said.

"I see you haven't distributed all of them yet." He chuckled. "Everyone charged up to bash the Bashers tomorrow?"

"Yup."

At that moment, Myriah hit a slow ground ball that went under the legs of Buddy, Hannie and Karen.

"Whoops!" Mr Natt said. "You must be working them too hard, Coach."

I was so happy when practice was over.

As Mr Natt bent my ear about the delivery schedule for the new equipment (and almost made me late for the BSC meeting), Mary Anne walked Druscilla home.

"You did great," Mary Anne said.

"No, I didn't," Dru replied.

"Well, did you have fun at least?"

Dru shook her head. "Not really."

"Ohhhhh, I'm sorry."

After that, Dru didn't talk much. She seemed kind of thoughtful and withdrawn.

Then, in front of Mrs Porter's house, Dru suddenly said, "You know, I'm having flute lessons at school. And this new neighbour, Anna, she helps me at home."

"That's great, Dru—"

"I know a boy who plays drums and a girl who plays trumpet. Maybe we could make a band. You know, for the Krushers."

That one caught Mary Anne by surprise. "A band?"

"They have cheerleaders, don't they?"

"Well, yes, but—"

"Then they should have a band!" Dru raced inside. "I'm going upstairs to practise!"

Mrs Porter appeared at the door, looking rather bemused. "How did Druscilla like playing softball?" she asked.

"I'm not sure," Mary Anne replied.

She imagined Druscilla tootling away in the on-deck circle, then stepping to bat with her flute.

A band. Druscilla had quite an imagination.

10th CHAPTER

"He did *what* to it?"

I couldn't have been hearing right.

It was Saturday morning, an hour before the start of World Series Game Number Two. Linny Papadakis was on the phone. He'd called to inform me he couldn't wear his uniform. It seemed that Noodle, the Papadakises' poodle, had just—well, let's put it this way, the uniform needed to be washed, probably more than once.

"Can I wear my old Krushers uniform?" he asked.

I sighed with frustration. "An ordinary tracksuit will be fine."

"*Yyyyyes!* Thanks, Kristy!"

Click!

I know, I know. I told them they couldn't play without uniforms. But what could I do? This was an emergency.

When Buddy called a few minutes later to say that his baby sister Marnie had been sick over *his* uniform (shirt, trousers and cap), I began to get suspicious.

Then Nicky Pike called to say his uniform gave him a rash. That was the last straw.

"Have you been talking to Buddy or Linny?" I asked.

"No," Nicky said.

"Well, wear the uniform to the game. Bring a change of clothes in case it bothers you."

"But that's not fair! Linny doesn't have to wear his!"

Aha!

You get the picture. The Nappy Rebellion had begun.

I was firm with Nicky. Wear it or else.

I hung up and then made a quick phone call to Mr Natt. I left a request for Dru's uniform on his answering machine.

Now I really had to run. I wolfed down breakfast, brushed my teeth and ran for the back door.

"Time to go, David Michael!" I called.

"He's at Abby and Anna's," Mum replied from the kitchen.

I'd been so busy that I hadn't even noticed he'd gone.

I stopped and turned around. "What's he doing there?" I asked.

"A little pre-practice practice with Abby," Watson said. "He was supposed to be back by now."

Pre-practice practice? What was *that* supposed to mean?

"I'll get him," I said, running out of the door.

I jogged up McLelland Road. In the distance I could hear Dru practising the flute. The sound didn't seem to be coming from Mrs Porter's house, though. As I approached the Stevensons' house, I saw that a little game was underway on the lawn. David Michael was pitching, Abby was catching, Hannie was batting and Linny was fielding. (Everyone was in uniform except Linny.) Now I was really miffed. What was Abby doing? Athletes don't play before a big game. They conserve their energy. They work on mental preparation. She was going to wear them out.

"Okay, David Michael, throw me the knuckleball," Abby was saying. She crouched into a catcher's position.

David Michael wound up and pitched. The ball flew out of his hand, straight upwards. It landed about a metre to his left.

108

Everyone started giggling.

"I said 'Throw a knuckleball,' not 'Be a knucklehead.'" Abby slapped her forehead, pretending to be exasperated.

"Er, I hate to interrupt," I said, "but we have a game to play."

Abby stood up, smiling. "Hi, Kristy! Is it time already?"

"Yes, it's time," I said, trying my hardest to be polite. "Where's Dru?"

"Practising with Anna in the garden."

"I'll get them," I said. "David Michael, you get ready. Hannie and Linny, we'll see you there." (The Papadakises were going to the game with their parents.)

"Can I go, too?" Abby asked.

I was polite. I kept my cool. "If you want," I replied.

"All *right*!" David Michael shouted.

I ran around to the Stevensons' garden. There, Anna and Dru were sitting side by side on a picnic bench. A paperback book was on the bench, too. Between the girls was a metal music stand holding a hefty-looking book. Dru was staring at the book and struggling to play scales.

"Excellent," Anna was saying. "And don't forget, the whole notes are *very* slow."

"Ahem! Excuse me," I said.

109

Anna looked up with a start. "Oh, wow! We went over time! Sorry, Kristy."

"That's okay," I replied.

Druscilla was beaming. "I can play an E major scale! Listen."

As she put the flute to her lips, I said quickly, "Later, Dru. I really want to hear it. Seriously. But we have to go."

"Oh, all right." With a pout, Dru began packing up her flute.

"You too, Anna," I said. "I mean, if you can. We need a big cheering section."

"All right," Anna replied.

As she picked up her paperback, I noticed the word *Season* in the title.

Cool. I once read a great baseball book called *Short Season*. "Is that good?" I asked.

Anna's eyes lit up. "Wonderful. I've read it twice. Would you like to borrow it?"

She held it out. I could see the full title now. It was *The Mozart Season.*

"Er, maybe some other time," I said.

When Dru had finished, we ran around to the front of the house and collected Abby and David Michael.

Dru made a quick stop next door to let Mrs Porter know she was going to the game. Then we took off.

"*That* practice was fun," David

Michael said, skipping along. "We played some backward ball. Can we do that sometime, Kristy?"

Backward ball, by the way, is just like ordinary softball, except you run backwards around the bases. During the softball season, we sometimes played it during practice. When we were feeling silly.

"Not before a big game, David Michael," I said.

"Rats!" he muttered. "Why are we always so serious?"

A Natt's Nappies van was parked by the field when we arrived. Mr Natt was unloading boxes from the back.

He was wearing a Natt's Nappies uniform. I kid you not. It was just like the kids' and mine, only much larger.

"Hey, there!" he called to us. "Surprise, surprise!"

David Michael ran to him, goggle-eyed. "Is this the new equipment?"

Mr Natt grinned proudly. "Yes, sir! And just in time for your victory today!"

Actually, the equipment wasn't a surprise to me. Mr Natt had told me the delivery date after that horrible, embarrassing practice he'd visited.

I helped him open the boxes. Inside was everything he'd promised—bats of different weights and lengths; a new, adjustable rubber tee; a little gizmo filled with a spring-loaded spool of twine and powdered chalk (for making base lines); a catcher's mask, chestpad and kneepads; new batting helmets; and a megaphone.

"*Testing, Testing!*" Mr Natt shouted into the megaphone. "*Presenting the new World Champions—the Natt's Nappies!*"

Mr Natt chuckled. Abby broke into hysterics. David Michael looked as if he was going to throw up.

The game? Frankly, I've blotted a lot of it out of my mind. I do remember the fierce look on Mr Natt's face when he saw that eight team members were wearing their uniforms inside out. And the sound of the Basher left fielder screaming, "NAPPIES! NAPPIES!" in an obnoxious, singsong voice. And Linny Papadakis, struggling like mad as I held him back from a fistfight.

But most of all, I remember the score, which was Bashers 24, Nappies 7.

Mr Natt's smile disappeared by about the third inning. He tried to remain optimistic and friendly throughout the game.

But the last thing he said to me before I left was, "Next time, I want *all* the players in proper uniform."

And he was not smiling.

11th CHAPTER

"I'll be at the Addisons' that day," Stacey said.

"I've got ballet," Jessi reminded me.

Claudia shrugged apologetically. "The Arnolds."

"Rosie Wilder," Mary Anne said. "And Logan has a game. I'm sorry."

"Well, *I'll* be there," Mallory said.

I love it when the Babysitters Club is busy. Really. That's the point of the club, right? But sometimes—just sometimes—I wish things would slow down.

It was Monday, two days after our Big Defeat. I had arranged a practice for Tuesday. An intensive practice. I told the players we'd work on the fundamentals. But I also offered to have a little game of backward ball, just to cheer them up. Anything to restore that old Krushers spirit.

114

The only problem was, I needed help. Practices are always better with BSC members around. Especially someone like Logan, who's so good at sports. Or Shannon, who's always gung-ho. Claudia and Mary Anne hardly know which end of the bat to hold, but they're good at following instructions and organizing the kids.

At least Mallory was going to be there. That was better than nothing. But only just. She always has her hands full with her siblings (and she hates sport even more than Mary Anne does).

Rrrring!

"Babysitters Club!" Jessi said, picking up the receiver. "Friday? I'll check and call you back, Mr Hill."

Looking at the calendar, Mary Anne frowned. "Uh-oh!"

"We're all booked?" Stacey asked.

Mary Anne nodded. "Except Logan and Shannon, and I know Logan can't miss practice the night before a game."

"I can call Shannon later, when she comes home from space cadets," Claudia said. "Call the Hills and tell them we'll be in touch tonight."

Even though we were one full member short, we hadn't yet missed a job. But we'd come awfully close. Mary Anne practically had to bribe Logan to persuade him to skip a football practice the Wednesday before. (He hates doing that. His teammates tease him so much about his membership of the BSC.)

No, I had not forgotten about the idea of a new member. I just hadn't had time to consider it. Not until the World Series was over. Besides, any day now the early autumn sitting rush was bound to ease up.

At least I hoped so.

At practice on Tuesday afternoon, I counted seven uniformed players.

Groan.

That was *fewer* than before. I was furious.

Did I scream and yell at the renegades? Throw them off the field? Hit them over the head?

I wanted to do all of the above. But I couldn't. First of all, I knew how bad they were feeling. I didn't want to lower their morale even more. Second, if I banished the non-uniformed players, we wouldn't have enough left for a team. That meant we'd have to forfeit the game.

And I would never do that. If we were going to lose to the Bashers, we'd do it with a fight.

Besides, Mr Natt wasn't there. And as

far as I knew, he had no plans to turn up.

So I did not explode. I was mature. Professional.

All I did was call a team meeting and tell the kids that whoever didn't wear a uniform on Saturday for the third game would not play.

That threat seemed to work.

"Okay, players look lively!" I shouted.

They shuffled back on to the field. You'd think they were going off to prison.

I tried to run a good practice. Really. You should have seen me. I hit so many grounders and pop flies that my thumbs chafed. I was coach, pitching instructor, head cheerleader and counsellor.

How did they do? Whoa! Home run derby! Double and triple plays galore. The Nappies were so full of team pride they begged me to let them run home for their uniforms.

Just kidding. Wishful thinking, I suppose.

The truth? The Nappies were more like Droopy Drawers.

When a couple of Bashers wandered by, things went from bad to worse. They hung around behind the third-base line, sniggering. Once or twice I heard someone mutter, "Dirty Nappies."

I don't know what they said to Nicky,

but at one point he took off after them, fists clenched. Luckily, they ran away and didn't come back.

I was breaking up a group of outfielders who were searching for four-leafed clovers, when I heard a familiar voice call out, "Pretedd you're a chimpadzee!"

I turned to see Abby behind home plate. She was dressed in a tracksuit, her hair was pulled back in a pony tail, and she held a softball in her right hand.

Terrific. Just what I needed before the biggest game of the season. Fooling around. "Abby, don't—" I began. I wanted to kill her.

"Cub od, guys, how does a chimpadzee walk?" she shouted.

The infielders spread their legs far apart and loped around, their fingertips scraping the ground. One of them started grunting, "Oooh-oooh-oooh!" and the rest followed.

"That's perfect!" Abby said. "Dow look where your glubs are. That's where they should be all the tibe—touching the dirt. Okay, here cubs a groudder."

She tossed the ball, on a bounce, towards the area between first and second.

Bobby, still imitating a chimp, scooped up the ball and threw it to first.

118

Smack. It landed right in first-baseman Linny's glove.

"Eeeeeee-ee-ee-ee!" Linny screeched, jumping up and down.

I took a deep breath. Okay, okay, it had worked. Gimmicks do, sometimes. But, seriously, you can't expect your infielders to grunt and scratch every time a ground ball is hit.

"Abby," I said patiently, "thanks for the help, but—"

Abby smiled. "I did't bead to butt id. Sorry. I was just waddering aroudd, add I saw the practice—"

That was all she said. Her eyes widened. Her face turned red. Out of her mouth came a strange wheezing noise.

"Abby, are you all right?" I asked.

Nodding weakly, Abby stumbled to her rucksack, which was lying in the grass beyond the on-deck circle. She reached into it and pulled out a small plastic pipe. Then she inserted one end in her mouth and inhaled.

After a few moments she sat against the backstop. "Asthma," she said with a thin smile. "I'm used to it. It looks worse than it is."

"Can I do something to help?"

"That's what I was going to ask you. I

119

thought you could do with a little help before the game."

I looked around. None of the kids seemed to have noticed what had happened. Most of them were still throwing the ball around like monkeys.

With lots of enthusiasm. And accuracy.

Gimmicks or not, having Abby around couldn't hurt.

She seemed healthier. Even her stuffed-up voice had cleared. "Are you sure you can handle it?" I asked.

"Of course! Hey, if I drop dead, bury me under the pitcher's mound." She grinned. "That was a joke."

"Okay," I said with a shrug. "Why not?"

"Yes? Shall I work on attack or defence?"

I spotted Patsy and Laurel near the first-base line, doing a little soft-shoe dance with their bats.

"Attack," I said. "I'll take the field."

Several players lined up in front of the Kuhn girls for batting practice. "Who's next?" Abby asked.

"Me," Dru replied.

"Hey, you pushed in!" Jackie said.

"I did not," Dru protested.

"You did!"

"Did not, Tacky Jackie!"

"Kristyyyyyyyyyy!"

"Hey, easy, Druscilla," Abby said.

Dru stuck out her chin. "Well, he wasn't paying attention, so he loses his turn."

"Ah, you're using American League rules," Abby said. "I'm used to National League rules. Even if the batter spaces out, he keeps his turn."

Huh?

It was ridiculous, and the kids knew it. But it stopped the argument, and it made them both smile.

Me, too, to tell you the truth.

"Choke up on the bat, Jackie," Abby instructed. "And try bending your knees a little more."

She ran to the pitcher's mound and tossed the ball to him. He swung and missed. Buddy, who was catching, threw the ball back.

"Spread your legs a little wider," Abby said, winding up for the next pitch. "Now, here comes a giant brussels sprout, heading right for your dinner plate. What are you going to do?"

Jackie's eyes lit up. "Yeeeeeeaaagh!" he cried.

Smack! He hit the ball up the first base line. Linny stopped it with his glove, and it bounced back towards home. Jackie, still

121

angry with the brussels sprout, chased after it with the bat. "Yeeeeeeaaagh!"

"Hey, watch it!" Linny shouted.

"Who-o-oa!" Abby ran to him and snatched the bat away.

(See what I mean about gimmicks?)

"Don't forget your safety rules!" I reminded them.

I have to say, practice became much better with Abby there. I was able to focus more attention on individuals.

I did have to tone her down sometimes, though. Especially when she tried to train players to step on the bases by imagining a cockroach on each one. It's one thing to be a natural athlete, but it's another to be an effective coach. Fun is fun. But you can't have a team of monkeys and cock-roach-stampers on the field.

Still, Abby had potential. She really knew how to break the tension. And the Krushers—I mean, Nappies—were starting to look more like their old selves.

Druscilla, however, was another story. I'd never seen her so sour and sullen. She kept snapping at the other players, stick-ing out her tongue, teasing the younger ones.

She really annoyed me. At last I saw her say something to Jamie Newton that made him storm off the field, crying and taking off his uniform shirt.

I stopped the practice. "What happened?" I asked Jamie.

"She called me a baby and said I should really wear nappies!" Jamie blurted out.

I looked at Dru. She was smirking.

What did I do? The only thing I could do. I benched her.

You know what she said? "I quit!" Just like that.

After that, and until the practice was over, she was nice as can be.

Honestly, I could not work her out.

12th CHAPTER

Thursday

Okay. I knew I was going to have to earn my way back into the Baby-sitters Club. You've seen me. I've been on my very best behavior. I haven't missed a single meeting or switched out of a job at the last minute. And I haven't asked for any special praise. Right?

Right.

Well, folks, after today I think I deserve the BSC Medal of Honour...

Stacey was exaggerating. About the Medal of Honour, that is.

But she was right about the other stuff. She was a model reinstated BSC member.

She was still going out with Robert, but the relationship was no longer her whole life. She was her old, non-snobby self.

When was Stacey's probation going to end? I didn't know. I had never put a time limit on it. But at the rate she was going, it would be soon.

That Thursday, Stacey was sitting for Dru. It was a last-minute job. You see, I had arranged a practice for that afternoon. Knowing Dru had joined the team, Mrs Porter had arranged a last-minute lunch date. But now that Dru had left the team, Mrs Porter was stuck.

Stacey to the rescue.

Dru was in her room, tooting away on the flute. Stacey walked in and smiled.

"I can play 'Row, Row, Row Your Boat'," Dru said. "It goes like this."

Stacey listened. It did sound like "Row, Row, Row Your Boat". Sort of. If you imagined it very slowly, all on one note, with a few squeaks thrown in.

"Great!" Stacey burst into applause.

"You mean, '*brava*'," Dru said. "You shout '*brava*' for girls and '*bravo*' for boys. That's what Anna says."

"Oh, sorry. *Brava!*"

"Thank you." Dru stood up and curtseyed. "Flute is really easy, you know. Anna taught me the right arm butcher. It's like this."

She spread her lips into a funny, flattened-out shape.

Huh? Stacey just smiled and nodded.

(Actually, Dru was trying to say *embouchure*, which means "the way you form your mouth when you play an instrument". We checked with Anna.)

"You know what?" Dru went on. "Scott Hsu tried to play my flute at school. He was so bad. But he says he's an expert on the kazoo. That's even easier than the flute. And this girl at Stoneybrook Day, Sheila Nofziger, has trumpet lessons. That's hard. And Moon Pinckney plays drums. That's enough for a band, isn't it?"

"Hmm, four kids?" Stacey said. "I suppose so. A small band. A quartet."

"Cool. Can we practise today? Please please please? The next game is on Saturday."

"Game? I thought you'd left the team."

"No. I was kicked out because I'm rubbish. Moon and Sheila are rubbish, too. They once played for the Nappies, when they were the Krushers, but Kristy kicked

126

them out, too. So we can all be in the Nappies official band, because Kristy won't let us join the team."

Stacey nodded. "All right. Give me those names again, and we'll make some phone calls."

Okay, I need to stop here for a moment. Don't think Stacey is a dope. She didn't believe a word of Dru's lies. Kicked out of the team? No way. Those other kids had been temporary substitutes for Krushers who were on holiday. I had offered them full-time slots when the players returned. But they had resigned, same as Dru.

Stacey has a theory for why Dru lied. She thinks Dru never wanted to play ball in the first place. Dru said I threw her off the team because she needed an excuse not to play, so that she could form her band. She was probably provoking me during practice.

(Well, all right. It sounds believable. Dru is going through a tough time. But still, I think Stace at least should have said something to Dru. I mean, a lie is a lie.)

Anyway, by about four-thirty, the musical rehearsal was underway.

Hoooooot! went Druscilla's flute.

Honnnk, Scott played on his kazoo.

Blaaat! squawked Sheila's trumpet.

CRRRRAAAAAAASH! That was Moon's cymbal. Yes, cymbal. His mum had driven him over in an estate car with his complete drum set.

It was definitely not Mozart Season in the Porter house.

"Er, very . . . good, everybody," said Maestro McGill. "But maybe you could try to play together, with some kind of rhythm. I'll move my arm to the beat, okay?"

Stacey raised her arm. The players watched intently. With a deep breath, she began.

Hoooooot!

Honnnk!

Blaaat!

CRRRRAAAAAAASH!

Uh, oh!

Have you ever seen *The Music Man*? I have. It's about this crooked salesman (who's secretly a good guy) who takes money from parents, saying he'll set up a boys' band. When he actually has to conduct the kids, he makes up something called the Think System. He turns to the band and says, "Okay, kids, *think* the 'Minute Waltz'."

Well, Stacey saw the show with me.

"Come on, you lot," she said, "*think* 'Row, Row, Row Your Boat'."

This time, the hoots, honks, blats and crashes had a kind of rhythm.

They played that until Stacey could stand it no longer. Then Dru insisted on trying "Mary Had a Little Lamb".

That one went better. Stacey said you could actually make out a tune, sort of. But then Scott started making *baaah*-ing noises with his kazoo every time they got to the "lamb" part of the song, and they laughed hysterically.

Practice that day, by the way, was a definite improvement. Abby asked if she could help again, and I let her. Almost all of the kids wore their uniforms (Linny claimed he'd lost his, and Buddy said he'd mistakenly used his to clean tar off the drive).

So I was in a pretty decent mood when I got home. Then I heard all the squawking next door, so I ran over there to see what was going on.

"Kristy!" Dru squealed when I walked in. "Listen to us!"

"They've really improved," Stacey insisted as they started playing again.

Improved? The noise almost curled my hair.

"Great!" I said.

"She likes us!" Dru cried out. "So can we be your official band, Kristy?"

Stacey was giving me a very sharp look. A *you'd-better-say-yes* look. Which, I thought, was pretty bold for a BSC member on probation.

But how could I say no? I'd never seen Dru so happy. "I'd be honoured," I replied.

"YEEEEAAAAAA!" the kids cheered.

"But wait!" Dru said. "What's our name?"

"The Official Band?" Moon suggested.

"Peanut Butter?" said Sheila.

"Huh?" Scott grunted.

Sheila shrugged. "It's something everybody likes.'

"I know!" Stacey volunteered. "The Krusher Quartet."

"Perfect," I said.

"But they're not the Krushers," Dru protested. "For Nappies you have to use an *N* word."

She thought for a moment. Then a huge smile spread across her face.

"I have it," she said. "Our official name is The Nasty Nappies!'"

Everyone giggled, and agreed that was the best.

Well, everyone but me. I still liked the Krusher Quartet.

13th
CHAPTER

"Atta girl, Patsy!" I yelled. "Good eye!"

"Come on, that was a *strike*!" complained the Basher pitcher.

"It was not!" Scowling, Patsy gripped the bat tightly.

Mr Natt leaned over to me. "Has anyone worked with her on the placement of her fingers?"

"Well, yes—"

But he was already heading towards home plate. "Sweetheart, hold the bat like this. . ."

Game three of the World Series was underway. It was the bottom of the second, and we were already losing 7–2. For the first time everyone was in uniform, which made me feel relieved. Also, Abby had offered to attend the game and help. That was nice, too. She didn't annoy me nearly as much as she used to.

Mr Natt, however, was another story.

He arrived just as the game was starting. He spent the first half of the inning chatting to the parents of the Nappies on the sidelines. Then he approached the parents of the Bashers. He picked up and played with every baby he saw. He handed out his card a lot.

Then he turned his attention to the game.

"Hold your arms *back*." Mr Natt pulled on Patsy's arms. "Now, don't splay those fingers." He pushed her fingers together on the bat. "There."

When Mr Natt had finished, Patsy looked like the Tin Woodsman in the *Wizard of Oz*, before Dorothy oils him. Awkward and stiff.

"Way to go, Patsy, way to go!" cried the Nappy cheerleaders.

She missed the next pitch by a mile.

"That's okay, Patsy," I said. "Keep it loose."

Patsy hit a weak grounder to first and was out.

Matt, our best hitter, was up next. He smashed a home run.

The Nappies and their crowd went wild. Mr Natt shouted, "Yes! What a swing!

132

You see, Patsy, if you'd been on first, it would have been a *two*-run homer!"

At the start of the next inning, Abby and I stood together on the Nappies' side, near Mr Natt. One of the Bashers hit a sharp line drive into centrefield. Jake was in a perfect position to field it, but it scooted under his legs.

"Run after it, Jakey!" I yelled.

He did. But by the time he threw the ball in, the batter had run all the way home.

"You were daydreaming, centre-fielder!" Mr Natt shouted.

Jake looked crushed.

The next Basher batter hit a screamer up the third base line. Hannie didn't have a chance at it.

"Bad positioning, third baseman!" Mr Natt called out to her.

"Player," said Abby.

Mr Natt smiled politely. "Excuse me?"

"Third base *player*," Abby repeated. "Hannie is not a third base*man*."

"Oh," said Mr Natt. "Of course."

Abby looked at me. I looked at her. We almost cracked up.

Well, we survived that inning pretty well, and the next one. But in the fourth inning, the Bashers scored eight runs. We were, to put it bluntly, horrible.

When the inning ended, the team looked as if they had given up.

"They're wiping you out!" was Mr Natt's comment as the team lined up to bat. "You don't want to lose, do you? You used to be winners!"

Ugh! Nothing like being positive, is there?

"That's all right," Abby butted in. "I saw a heads-up play in right field that cut off a run, right, Bobby?"

Bobby grinned. "I went like *this* with my glove, but the ball went like *this*, so I had to go like *this*!" He pantomimed the play.

"And that was a great dive at short-stop, Karen!" I said. "You almost got it."

Karen looked sheepish. From the dive, the front of her uniform shirt was covered with dirt.

"I suppose that makes you our first official Dirty Nappy," Abby remarked.

The kids laughed.

"Harrumph!" said Mr Natt. "Who's up?"

Suzi Barrett shuffled to the plate.

Well, Mr Natt had plenty of advice for Suzi. And for the next batter, and the next.

None of it helped. In fact, I'd never

seen the Krusher/Nappies play so badly. Their hearts just weren't in it.

I tried to keep their spirits up. My coaching philosophy is: build up, don't knock down. Reward good playing. Avoid the word *Don't*. And Abby was with me one hundred per cent.

But Mr Natt kept putting his two cents in. He began calling for all kinds of fancy strategies—hit-and-run plays, fielding at double-play depth, sacrifice bunts. None of the kids knew what on earth he was talking about.

Towards the end of the game, he became more and more frustrated. He called Margo a slowcoach. He told Nicky he'd "never make the majors". None of this helped the quality of playing.

Our cheerleaders kept trying to start a rally, but even they gave up after a while.

The final score was Bashers 30, Nappies 9.

You have never seen a glummer-looking lot of kids. As they dragged their feet towards the sidelines, they didn't say a word to each other.

"Okay, guys, let's do the Basher cheer!" I said.

We did, but it sounded more like a loud mumble.

My team definitely needed a pep talk.

Mr Natt was off shaking parents' hands, so now was the perfect time.

I gathered the kids around. Then I took a deep breath and beckoned Abby over, too. "Okay, we're behind two games to one," I said. "But we're not out of it yet."

"Far from it," Abby added. "And I know you lot can do better. I saw some great plays out there."

"And some good run-scoring," I said. "With a little work, we'll be back to our brand of Krusher ball."

Oops! The word *Krusher* had flown out of my mouth. And just as Mr Natt was walking towards us.

He was smiling, sort of. "Team meeting, eh?" he said. "Good. We need one. You know, this isn't the team I saw in that first game, boys and girls. *That* team had guts. *This* one was weak. This one decided to give up without a try."

Abby and I gave each other a Look.

"You have the best uniforms, the best equipment," Mr Natt went on. "So what happened? You all just rolled over and played dead. I'm not here to sponsor losers. Is that what you are, losers?"

The Nappies' heads were drooping.

"Prove me wrong," he went on. "Win the next game. Give it all you've got. Because if you don't, the series is over!

Understand?" He let his words hang in the air for a moment, like a bad smell, and then said, "Okay, see you next week, kids. Oh, and one thing. Those uniforms look terrific, so keep them nice and clean."

The players slunk away. Half of them looked as if they were going to cry.

I was numb. Stunned. Was this what a sponsor was supposed to do?

With a half smile Mr Natt turned to Abby and me. "You have to get their attention, you know. Give them a little nudge now and then.'

"Nudge?" Abby repeated. "That was no nudge. That was like hitting them with a sledgehammer."

Mr Natt's smile vanished.

My jaw nearly hit the first base line.

She was joking. Had to be. I looked at her, hoping for a punchline.

"I beg your pardon?" Mr Natt asked.

"Did you think you were inspiring them or something?" Abby asked. "You have been awful to them all day. No wonder they lost. And after that little talk, I'd be surprised if they ever want to pick up a softball again."

I was speechless. I could feel the blood draining from my face.

"I—well, you certainly have your

opinions, don't you?" Mr Natt said. "When *you* sponsor a team one day, I'm sure you'll handle it your way. I happen to know what my team needs."

"Your team?" Abby shot back. "It's *Kristy's* team. And they don't need you, Mr Natt. They were doing just fine without you. Right, Kristy?"

Earth to Kristy.

They were both glaring at me.

My heart was racing. "I suppose. I mean, we were doing okay."

Mr Natt let out a snort. "Yes, with your battered equipment and ragged uniforms. And then I came along and made you look professional, gave you the top-notch treatment you deserved. And for free, if I may remind you, young lady. It was all at my expense."

"Well, it wasn't really free, Mr Natt," I said. "I mean, before you came along we didn't have nice things. But we did have a name we liked, the Krushers. And we had lots of fun. And no outsider told us what to do. We had to give all that up, didn't we?"

"That was your choice," Mr Natt said.

I nodded. "You're right."

It *was* my choice, and I knew it. But Mr Natt had never told me he'd planned to take over the team. He never said our players would have to wear uniforms with daft-looking logos. If I'd known those things, I'd never have made that "choice".

"Well, then," Mr Natt said briskly, "I'm glad we—"

"And it's my choice to give you your things back," I said.

Mr Natt looked at me as if I'd just spoken to him in Greek. Abby was beaming.

"We *don't* need you, Mr Natt," I said firmly. "We'll return the uniforms, and you can take the equipment now."

I thought Mr Natt was going to explode. His mouth flapped open and shut a few times. Then, at last, he said, "Very well. My best wishes for the remaining games."

We left him there to pack the stuff in his van.

My knees were shaking. "Did I say that?" I whispered.

"He deserved it," Abby whispered back. "You did the right thing, Coach."

"You, too. You were great." I grinned. And suddenly I knew exactly what to do next, too. "Abby, the kids love you. Would you like to be my assistant coach?"

Abby put her arm around my shoulder.

"I suppose that means I'm an official Krusher."

"Yes!"

Krushers. Kristy's Krushers. It's such a cool name.

14th CHAPTER

When Linny heard the news, he was ecstatic. So ecstatic that he celebrated by throwing his Nappies' uniform on the barbecue.

It's a good thing Mr Papadakis caught him. Linny was grounded for the rest of the week.

Well, he was given parole on one afternoon, the Tuesday afternoon of our fourth World Series game against the Bashers.

Which we won, 19–17.

Yes, folks. You heard me right. Yyyyooooourrr Krrrrusherrrrrs were on the march! The series was tied, two games to two.

What a difference. Our old bats felt just great. And it was so nice to see *Krushers* on those ragged shirts.

Abby, by the way, was a real champ. She bandaged a few scrapes, coached the runners and batters and fielders well, and soothed a couple of sore egos.

Bart, however, was not happy. At the end of the game he told me I should phone Mr Natt and apologize. He said I should support local businesses, that I owed it to the community to be sponsored by Natt's Nappies.

Uh-huh. He just wanted us to stay depressed and beatable.

What a dork. (But I still like him.)

The final, deciding game was on Saturday.

I was so excited I could hardly sleep the night before. Two slices of grapefruit were all my stomach could handle for breakfast.

Okay, so we had won on Tuesday. We'd been in great spirits. Back to normal. But I was still worried.

We had been un-Nappied for only a week. What if Mr Natt had left permanent psychological scars? What if our win had been a fluke? What if some of the Krushers still thought of themselves as Nappies in their hearts?

Do you think I was going overboard?

Mrs Stevenson drove seven of us to the game. That's right, seven. Abby, David

Michael, me—and the four members of the Krusher Quartet! (They, too, had officially changed their name.)

Yes, our band was making its debut. Moon and Scott were wearing jackets and ties. Dru and Sheila were dressed in brand-new outfits.

Anna was going to meet us there. She had been appointed the conductor of the quartet.

I wasn't so sure the band was a great idea. Especially as we already had cheerleaders. I thought all the noise might be distracting.

Abby called me a worrywart.

Besides, Dru looked so happy. I decided to go with the flow.

The sidelines filled up soon after we arrived. It seemed as if half of Stoneybrook had turned out for the big event. Our cheerleaders were thrilled to have a band on the sidelines. Every time they performed a cheer, Moon banged out the beat.

The Bashers got off to a quick 3–0 start in the top of the first.

But when the Krushers came to bat, we released our secret weapon: "Row, Row, Row Your Boat".

The Bashers didn't know what had hit them. Half the infielders were trying not to laugh. The pitcher looked as if he had a stomach-ache.

Bart asked me, "Is this *legal*?"

I said, "I think it *is*."

He was not amused.

By the fourth inning the score was 10–10. Matt had hit his usual two home runs. Linny hit one, too, and Jake contributed a bases-loaded triple.

Each big hit, of course, was an excuse for the band to play. They alternated their song list well throughout the game. Which wasn't hard to do with only two songs.

(It wasn't until Jake's triple that I realized the band's other song was "Mary Had a Little Lamb". I'd thought it was "Twinkle, Twinkle, Little Star".)

Abby was fantastic. She knew just how far to push each player. She praised them when they deserved it, encouraged them when they made a mess of things. No one missed Mr Natt.

But the Bashers weren't playing dead. They kept pulling ahead of us. When we came to bat in the bottom of the last inning, we were losing 23–19.

Did I tell you Jackie Rodowsky's nickname was The Walking Disaster? Well, it is. And for good reason.

He led off the inning by sneezing as the pitch was hurtling toward him. His whole body jerked forward. The ball hit him on his behind.

"Ow!" he cried.

"Hit by pitch. Runner takes first base!" the ref commanded. (That's a rule of the game.)

The next batter was Margo Pike. She smacked the ball past the first base player. The Bashers right fielder ran to field it— and fell.

Margo was in shock. She stood rooted to first base.

"Go! Go!" Abby and I shouted.

She did. All the way home (where she collided with Jackie).

Now the score was 23–21, Bashers.

After a couple more hits and a couple of outs, Hannie Papadakis was up with two runners on base.

"Oh, no!" David Michael groaned. "Can't Matt be up?"

I glared at him.

"At least I'm not clumsy like you!" Hannie snapped.

"No, you're just ugly," David Michael retorted.

"Yeah, well, the baseball is your head! Watch me hit it."

"I'm really worried."

"Remember, you're teammates," I said.

But Hannie was fuming. She gritted her teeth. The pitcher tossed the ball. She swung.

David Michael's head went sailing into short centre field.

Hannie dug in. She ran around first. She ran around second. She ran around third.

The Bashers were throwing the ball all over the place—to everywhere Hannie had just been.

"Throw it home! Throw it home!" Bart shouted.

The ball bounded towards home plate. The catcher crouched. Hannie flew towards him.

"Out of my way!" she commanded.

The catcher flinched. The ball bounced into his glove—and back out.

Hannie charged home.

The cheerleaders screamed. Forget about a victory song. The band just started honking and squawking and banging. Parents and babysitters were yelling. Players hugged each other and jumped up and down.

Abby and I were practically crying, we were so happy.

We had done it. We had won the championship all by ourselves.

Who needed Nappies, anyway?

After the game, Watson and Mum gave a small neighbourhood party. Linny and Hannie came to it, and so did Karen, Andrew, Abby, Anna, Shannon Kilbourne and the members of the Krusher Quartet. Even Bart turned up (I told you he was a good sport).

While we were munching away and talking, Abby banged on a glass to silence everyone.

"I would like to toast Kristy Thomas," she said, "who knows when it's time to be out of nappies!"

"Here, here!" Watson said.

Everyone cheered. Except Emily Michelle. She just looked at Nannie and said, "Kristy? Na-pee?"

It was a fantastic party. But I felt a bit sad. I wished the season could start all over again.

At the end of the party, Druscilla walked over to me with a grave expression. "Kristy," she said. "Um, I hope you're not angry with me. . ."

Uh-oh!

"What, Dru?"

"Well, our group decided we want to keep playing together," she said. "But now that the games are over, we can't be the Krusher Quartet any more. It doesn't

147

make sense. So we're Druscilla and the Dynamos. Is that okay?"

"Dru," I said, "I think I can deal with it."

She left the house happily chattering away to Scott, Moon and Sheila about future plans.

Seeing that, I think, was my favourite part of the party.

15th CHAPTER

"Order!" I called out. "Okay, sit down! I have some new business!"

I could hardly wait to speak.

The idea had struck me after the party. I could not believe I hadn't thought of it before.

"Listen, everyone! Our problems are solved," I said. "I propose, for our new members, Abby and Anna Stevenson!"

(What did I tell you? Was that perfect or what?)

I didn't wait for a response. "They are both very responsible," I continued. "Anna has been giving flute lessons to Druscilla, and Abby has been a terrific assistant coach for the Krushers. And they love kids. That's obvious. Also, we know them and we like them. I say they're in."

"Er, could you stop beating around the bush, Kristy?" Claudia asked. "How do you feel about them?"

"Ha ha," I said. "I hereby move we ask them to join."

"Hallelujah!" Shannon said. "The girl has come to her senses. I thought you'd never find another member."

"Do you think we really need two, though?" Claudia asked.

"Oh, yes, absolutely," Shannon said quickly. "I second the motion."

"Hang on a minute," Stacey interrupted. "What about Abby's asthma? What if she had an attack while sitting?"

Mary Anne nodded. "It wouldn't be safe, Kristy."

"What if you have an insulin reaction, Stacey?" I asked.

"That's why I carry raisins with me, and packets of honey," Stacey replied.

"And Abby takes an inhaler wherever she goes," I explained. "I've already asked her."

Now even Mary Anne and Stacey looked satisfied. "Okay, all in favour?" I asked.

Mary Anne, Stacey, Shannon, Claudia and my hands shot up.

"What about you two?" I asked Jessi and Mal.

150

"Well," Jessi said tentatively, "we don't really know the twins."

"Fair enough," I said. "I'll invite them to the next meeting."

Two days later, just before 5:15 pm, Charlie drove the twins and me to Claud's house. (I had called the meeting fifteen minutes early, so we could all get acquainted.) By the way, Abby and Anna did not complain about the car (Charlie's beloved old wreck), which was a very good sign.

I hadn't told them exactly why they were invited. I just hinted it would be a good way to get to know the BSC members.

When we walked into Claud's room, everyone was already there.

How did the meeting go? It was as if the Stevenson twins had been members from the beginning. Abby sat on Claud's bed. Anna sat cross-legged near Jessi. (I could hear those two talking on and on about Stravinsky music, or something equally exciting.)

At one point I crouched down next to Jessi and Mal. Anna was now talking to Stacey, and Abby to Mary Anne.

"So?" I said. "Is it unanimous?"

With big grins, they gave me thumbs-up signs.

I called the meeting to order at five-thirty.

"For our first order of business," I announced, "as founder and chairman of the Babysitters Club, I hereby extend an official offer of membership to Abby and Anna Stevenson."

As quickly as I could, I explained the rules, meeting times and operating procedures. I told them they'd be alternative officers, which meant they'd be stand-ins whenever another officer was absent. I was dying to hear their responses.

The sisters glanced at each other. Next to them, Claudia was beaming. Mary Anne had tears in her eyes. (To tell you the truth, I'd been a bit worried about Mary Anne. I mean, Abby and Anna were replacing her *sister*. And you know how sensitive Mary Anne is.)

"Well—I—wow!" Abby stammered. "That's so nice of you." She shrugged. "Yes! I suppose. Thank you!"

Abby Stevenson at a loss for words? I thought I'd never see the day.

Anna sighed. "Well, I'm really happy you asked," she said. "And I do like baby-sitting, very much. But I have to say no."

No?

"Are you serious?" The words were out of my mouth before I could think.

"The thing is," Anna replied. "I'll be really busy after school. I have violin lessons and orchestra rehearsals, and there's this competition I need to prepare for in November. Besides, I like to have a couple of hours to practise before dinner on school days. And that's when you lot meet." She shrugged. "Sorry. But thanks."

I don't think any of us had expected that response. I know I hadn't. I suppose I thought no one would turn down such an offer.

"Well, okay," I said eventually. "We understand. And if you change your mind, the offer will still be open."

Anna nodded.

Abby? She looked like a Christmas tree.

"Two, four, six, eight!" I shouted.

"Who do we appreciate?" the other BSC members joined in. "*Abby! Abby! Hurrah!*"

We burst into applause. Well, all except Mary Anne. She was the very first one to give Abby a hug. "Welcome to the Baby-sitters Club," she said softly.

We had a great meeting that day. Abby went through a blow-by-blow description of our argument with Mr Natt, playing all the roles. I was laughing so hard, I thought I'd choke on my biscuits.

That evening, our family had the Stevensons, Mrs Porter and Dru over for dinner. Anna and Dru played a piano-flute duet for us (luckily, they kept it short).

I loved having new friends in the neighbourhood. And I cannot tell you how good I felt two days later when I sat in my director's chair in Claudia's room for our Friday BSC meeting. Just the right number of people were sitting in the right places. Except now I saw a mass of dark curls where Dawn's white-blonde hair used to be.

Claudia's clock clicked to 5:30.

"Harrumph!" I said. "I call this meeting of the Babysitters Club to order with an official welcome to our newest member, Abby Stevenson!"

"Hurrah!" the others shouted.

Abby cleared her throat. She looked rather embarrassed. "And I hereby, um, officially wish to express my gratefulishness to the members—"

Rrrrrring!

Formalities were over. It was time to put Abby to work.